Bachelor's Bought Bride

JENNIFER LEWIS

MILLS
BOON®

First published in Great Britain 2011
Large Print edition 2011
Harlequin Mills & Boon Limited,
Eton House, 18-24 Paradise Road,
Richmond, Surrey TW9 1SR

© Harlequin Books SA 2010

Special thanks and acknowledgment are given to
Jennifer Lewis for her contribution to the
KINGS OF THE BOARDROOM series.

ISBN: 978 0 263 22257 9

JENNIFER LEWIS

has been dreaming up stories for as long as she can remember and is thrilled to be able to share them with readers. She has lived on both sides of the Atlantic and worked in media and the arts before she grew bold enough to put pen to paper. Happily settled in England with her family, she would love to hear from readers at jen@jen-lewis.com. Visit her website at www.jenlewis.com

For Julie,
international woman of mystery
and passionate San Franciscan,
who's made living in England
so much fun.

Acknowledgements:

Many thanks to the kind people who read the book while I was writing it, including Anne, Anne-Marie, Carol, Cynthia, Jerri, Leeanne, Marie and Paula, my agent Andrea and Senior Editor Krista Stroever.

<u>One</u>

Uh-oh. What now?

Bree Kincannon's father waved to her from across the ballroom. A self-conscious everyone-is-watching wave. She stiffened as he headed toward her, marching through the splendidly attired crowd. He'd left their table the moment dessert was done, heading out to see and be seen, as usual.

Bree, as usual, had settled into her chair to listen to the music and wait for the evening to end. She'd come only because the fundraiser was for one of her favorite charities.

Wary, she glanced up as her father approached, his silver hair gleaming in the ballroom lights. Then she noticed the tall man behind him.

Oh, no. Not another introduction. She thought he'd finally given up trying to introduce her to every eligible bachelor in San Francisco.

"Bree, dear, there's someone I'd like you to meet."

A familiar refrain. She'd heard it a lot in her twenty-nine years, and it rarely led beyond an awkward first date.

Still, she rose to her feet and planted a smile firmly on her lips.

"Gavin, this is my daughter, Bree. Bree, this is Gavin Spencer. He's an advertising executive with Maddox Communications."

Gavin Spencer thrust out his arm. She politely extended her hand to meet his. "Nice to..." *Oh, goodness.* She looked up and her heart almost stopped. Thick dark hair swept back from a high forehead. The slightest hint of five-o'clock shadow enhanced chiseled features, which framed a wide, sensual mouth.

He was gorgeous.

"Meet me?" A twinkle of humor lit warm gray eyes.

"Uh, yes. Really nice to meet you." She snatched her hand back. Her palm was practically sweating. Her father must be nuts thinking a man like this might be interested in her. "Maddox has done some really good campaigns lately. The print ads for Porto Shoes were really eye-catching."

And perhaps I could use the word really *a few more times in quick succession.* She felt her face heat.

"Thanks, I worked on that campaign." A smile revealed perfect white teeth. His chin had a slight cleft. "Your father tells me you're a photographer."

Bree's eyes darted to her father. He had? Shock and pride swept over her. He never bothered to say a word about her *hobby,* as he'd called it once. "Yes. I enjoy taking photos."

"She just won an award," her father chimed in,

his face beaming with bonhomie. "The Black Hat or something."

"Black B-Book," she stammered. "It's a commercial photography competition."

"I know what the Black Book Awards are." Gavin tilted his head. "That's quite an accomplishment."

Bree's father waved to someone across the ballroom, nodded his apologies and strode off into the crowd.

Leaving her all alone with the most breathtakingly handsome man in the room.

She swallowed, smoothed the front of her crinkled taffeta dress and wished she'd worn something less…hideous.

"What kind of photographs do you take?"

"Portraits, mostly." Her voice sounded reasonably steady, which was impressive under the circumstances. She was annoyed that this gorgeous man her father had forced on her was having such an effect on her. She always felt so out of place in these situations. "I try to capture people's personalities."

"That sounds like quite a challenge."

"It's mostly about timing. Picking the right moment." She shrugged. She couldn't explain it herself. "I think the technical term is that I have a knack for it."

His finely cut mouth widened into a smile and those dreamy gray eyes twinkled. "A knack generally implies the kind of talent that makes you stand out from the crowd."

"Well, I certainly don't stand out from this crowd." She swept her arm, indicating San Francisco's most elegant and well-heeled partygoers—and instantly regretted her foolish words.

Of course she stood out. As the frumpiest and most unexciting person there.

"Everyone here is trying so hard to stand out." Dimples appeared under his impressive cheek-bones. "It's the people who aren't trying who are more interesting. Would you like to dance?"

"Dance?" Did he mean with him? No one ever asked her to dance at these things.

"Is there an echo in here?"

"No. I mean, yes. Yes, I'd like to dance."

For a split second she wished the polished parquet would swallow her whole. Which would be quite a big gulp. Of course he didn't want to dance with her. He was just being polite. No doubt he'd have appreciated it if she politely refused.

But he extended his arm, clad in a deep black suit—like every other man at the formal gala— and led her to the dance floor where a band, in white tie and tails, played the thirties classic "In the Mood."

Gavin swept her out into the middle of the floor and slid his arm around her waist. Her whole body shivered with awareness, even through all the layers of crunchy taffeta. The steps to the dance were probably lodged somewhere in her subconscious. Lord knows she'd been dragged to enough dancing classes as a kid.

The room rushed past her as Gavin twirled her into a spin. He chased the music across the room, guiding them effortlessly through the other dancers. His enticing masculine scent wrapped around her, hypnotic and intoxicating. Her feet followed his almost as if they were attached, stepping in time. Her arm barely reached around his broad shoulders—which was quite something considering she was five feet nine inches—but she seemed to float along with him, gliding on the soaring trombones and quick-stepping with the punchy trumpets, until the music slid to a close.

Breathless and blinking, Bree extricated herself from Gavin's strong arms. Was that really her whipping around the floor like that—with a man like him?

"You're a wonderful dancer." His breath felt hot on her ear.

"Me? It was all you. I just had to follow."

"That's an art in itself. I bet you half the women in this room would be fighting so hard to lead they'd trip me up."

Bree laughed. "Probably true."

"You have a beautiful smile."

"Six years of orthodontics will do that for you."

He laughed. "And a wicked sense of humor." He led her off the dance floor, toward the bar. Eyes swiveled to him from all directions—both male and female eyes. Apparently no one could keep their gaze off the most impressive man in the room.

And he walked with his arm threaded firmly through hers.

Bree blinked under the unfamiliar glare of attention. They probably all wondered what on earth he was doing with her.

Heck, she wondered, too.

Being an heiress, and a plain one at that, made it easy to figure out what a man wanted. Begins with *m* and ends in *y*. But this guy could probably marry any heiress in the room—and there were plenty of them here tonight.

What was so special about her?

A voice in her head told her to stop worrying about it and just enjoy the attention that was making her heart beat faster than it had in quite some time.

"Would you like champagne?" He turned to offer her a glass.

"Thanks." Why not? The dance alone was something to celebrate. She took a sip and let the bubbles tickle her tongue.

He leaned in until his sexy stubble almost brushed her cheek. "How come I've never met you before?"

"I don't go out much. I adopted my two cats from the Oakland Animal Society, though, so I wanted to come to their fundraiser tonight. Do you have any pets?"

He shook his head. "Don't have the time. I work long hours and travel a lot. I bet your cats were lucky to find you."

"I like to think so. Especially since Ali needs insulin shots every day. Animals with health issues are hard to find homes for."

"You're a caring person."

"Or a sucker." She smiled. "But a happy one. They're my babies."

An odd expression flickered across Gavin's

face. Something in his eyes, really, since his chiseled features didn't move.

Was he wondering why he was wasting time with a cat-owning spinster in a puffy dress, while stunning women cast suggestive glances over their drinks at him?

She'd rather be home with her cats anyway. Being around Gavin made her nervous, had her analyzing every move he made. She'd be a lot more comfortable with a camera lens between them. He was definitely too good-looking. It couldn't be healthy for her insides to be fluttering like this.

"I'm here because a client bought a table for the agency. It's obviously a good cause but I don't like these dos much, either," he murmured. "Too many people. Long speeches. Chewy beef." His dimples appeared again.

A warm sensation filled her chest. "What do you like to do?"

He hesitated a moment. "Interesting question. I spend so much time working, sometimes I forget what else is out there." He smiled, sheepish.

"Lately though, I find myself wanting to slow down, enjoy the ride a bit more. Maybe even…" He paused and shoved a hand through his hair, as if embarrassed. "Settle down and start a family." His mouth formed a wry grin. "I guess that sounds sappy."

"Not at all." The way he looked at her with those soulful gray eyes made Bree feel woozy. Could this guy be more of a fantasy? "I think it's perfectly natural. Everyone needs balance in their life."

"Speaking of which, would you like to dance again? This song is one of my favorites."

The band had struck up a sultry Latin tune. Adrenaline prickled through her at the prospect of moving in sync with this man again. Was he for real?

Gavin entwined his arms with Bree's and led her back to the dance floor. He wished he wasn't wearing the stiff suit so he could feel her soft skin against his. So far everything about Bree seemed soft—the big gray eyes half hidden behind her glasses, her pink-tinged cheeks, her pretty, kissable mouth. He suspected there was also a soft, lush body hidden somewhere under all that crispy gray taffeta.

Her father had implied that she was unattractive and undesirable, and that her continued spinsterhood was a social embarrassment to him. His own daughter, a burden he'd pay well to be rid of. Could Elliott Kincannon really feel that way about the sweet woman on his arm?

Pure pleasure rippled through him as he slid his arm around her waist. Yes, she definitely had the kind of body a man could lose himself in. Full breasts bumped gently against his chest as he pulled her close. Her brown hair was pulled back into a tight knot and he wondered what it would look like cascading over her shoulders.

He liked the way she moved, too. Soft—again—and yielding, allowing her body to flow with his. Light on her feet as he twirled her slowly to the gentle rhythms. As she spun around to meet him, her eyes sparkled and she flashed a sweet, shy smile.

He couldn't help but respond with a smile of his own.

If first impressions were correct, then Bree Kincannon could make a very nice Mrs. Gavin Spencer. She might not be the kind of girl men flocked around in a bar, but so what? He didn't need some nipped-and-tucked trophy wife to prove his manhood.

And Bree Kincannon came with some very real incentives. One million of them, in fact.

Their eyes met again and a needle of guilt pricked his heart.

Could he really marry a woman for money?

He'd busted his ass for ten long years trying to build a reputation as a top-flight account executive. Since his first day on the job he knew he wanted to open his own agency. Bring together top creative talent, innovative thinking and creative media buying that would take the advertising world by storm.

If you'd told him ten years ago that he'd still be working for someone else at age thirty, he'd have laughed in your face.

But life had done a little laughing of its own.

His dad's pension plan had gone bust and he'd bailed his parents out of a mortgage mess. In truth, though, he was glad he could help them. The biggest mistake of his life was being dumb enough to trust a renowned "investment advisor" with a large chunk of his precious nest egg—only to learn in the papers it had been squandered on racehorses and vintage violins.

Gavin tugged Bree closer, enjoying the soft swell of her chest against his. Her long eyelashes lifted to reveal shining eyes.

He liked those eyes and it wasn't hard work to imagine looking at them for the rest of his life. He had a good feeling in his gut about Bree Kincannon, and his gut rarely steered him wrong.

Finding a wife, or even a girlfriend, had never been a priority for him. Married to his job, that's what his friends joked. True, though. He really loved his work and was more than satisfied with the occasional fling. At least then, no one was disappointed.

If he went through with this crazy plan, he'd work hard not to disappoint Bree. He'd be a good husband to her.

He dipped her slightly, and she yielded to the motion, letting herself fall backward into his hand. Trusting. She had absolutely no idea what was going through his mind. If she knew, she'd be appalled beyond belief.

But she wouldn't know. Ever.

She giggled as he pulled her back up. A rare flash of excitement flared in his chest. She was enjoying this and dammit, so was he. He twirled her around, holding her close, hand pressed to the inviting curve of her hip.

He had a good feeling about this whole thing.

Bree stood in front of the mirror in the powder room on the pretext of rearranging her hair. Really she just wanted to see what exactly Gavin Spencer was looking at with that gleam of interest in his eyes.

People always told her she had pretty eyes.

Rather an odd observation, since she wore glasses. She lowered the frames—the nice, low-profile ones she saved for special occasions—and peered into her own eyes. They didn't look all that special to her. Maybe that's what people said when they couldn't think of something else to compliment. She pushed the frames back up her nose where they settled comfortably into place. People said she should wear contacts but they were far too much hassle for her taste.

Her hair was a disaster, as usual. Unmanageable, frizzy and fighting her every step of the way. She never should have taken out the hairsticks she'd managed to jam in earlier. With a struggle, she poked them back in and secured a messy bun.

There wasn't a lick of makeup on her face, but then she never wore it. She wasn't skilled at applying lipstick, blush and eyeliner, so on the rare occasions she'd attempted to use them, she ended up looking like a clown.

And the dress was awful. Her Aunt Freda had assured her it "hid her figure flaws." It could also hide an international terrorist organization and several cases of contraband whiskey in its crispy folds. The boat neck turned her somewhat decent cleavage into an intimidating mountain range.

She didn't look any better than usual. If anything, she looked worse.

So why did Gavin seem so…entranced by her? Like he couldn't take his eyes off her. He'd guided her around the room since the moment they were introduced. She kept expecting him to spot someone else and bid her adieu, but he didn't.

In fact, she half suspected he was standing right outside the ladies room waiting for her.

She blew out hard. Bright patches of color illuminated her cheeks in a way that wasn't entirely charming. Her eyes were certainly shining, though.

As well they might be. She'd never danced like that. Even in her imagination! How could she not feel like Cinderella at the ball?

Which was funny, really, considering she was

one of the richest women in San Francisco. Of course she'd come by that money the old fashioned way—by inheriting it—so she wasn't proud of her wealth. Quite the opposite, in fact. She often imagined people clucking and muttering, "All that money, and look how little she's accomplished."

Her father certainly felt that way. Even said it once or twice.

She sucked in a long, deep breath and tucked a stray lock of wild hair behind her ear.

Bree Kincannon, you are a desirable and enticing woman.

Nope. Not convincing.

Bree Kincannon, you are a damned good photographer and a fantastic cat mom.

Better.

She half-smiled at her reflection, then wiped her smile away when she realized the sylph-like blonde beside her was staring. She quickly patted her hair and turned to the exit.

Outside there was no sign of Gavin. The little shock of disappointment surprised her. Then she chastised herself. Did she really expect a man like that to wait around for her like a faithful dog?

He was probably already dancing with someone else.

Surreptitiously she scanned the dance floor. Past midnight, so the crowd was thinning. All the men were dressed alike in black tie, but she knew she'd spot Gavin immediately. He had that kind of presence.

A tiny shimmer of relief trickled through her when she didn't see him.

But did that mean he'd left without saying goodbye? She'd probably never see him again. Why would he call her, of all people?

She lifted her chin and started to weave through the tables to where she'd sat with some of her father's duller business associates, which wasn't a very charitable way to think of them since they'd all been nice enough to pony up a thousand dollars per seat. She was relieved to see that they'd all left, and she lifted her beaded bag off the back of her chair and slung it over her taffeta-clad shoulder.

Another quick glance revealed no sign of Gavin. Cold settled in her stomach. So that was it. A lovely evening. A fantastic time.

Possibly the best night of her life.

She swallowed. No doubt everyone who'd stared at her on Gavin's arm was looking at her now, the same way they always did. Poor old Bree. Perennial wallflower.

She shuffled toward the exit. She usually got a cab home from these things as her father often stayed late to schmooze into the wee hours. Of course it was kind of pathetic that she still lived in the family mansion. But she loved Russian Hill, and the big attic studio she'd turned into her private apartment was filled with special memories of the happy years before her mom died. She used to paint there every afternoon, while Bree played on the floor near her easel.

Bree bit her lip. She was happy with her life. Really! She didn't need some tall, dark, handsome charmer to waltz in and stir up trouble.

She retrieved her coat from the cloakroom and slid it over her shoulders. She was just about to walk across the marble foyer toward the exit when her heart slammed to a halt.

Gavin. Tall and proud as a ship's mast, an earnest look on his chiseled features.

And he was talking to her father.

Bree frowned. How did they know each other so well? Her father usually bothered only with mega-wealthy entrepreneurs who could make him a fast and large buck. If Gavin was just an advertising executive—a challenging and inter-esting job, but still a job—why was her father leaning in to speak with him as if he was Bill Gates?

She pulled her coat about herself and started slowly toward them. They both looked up fast when they noticed her, which made a weird knot of anxiety form in her belly.

"Bree, darling!" Her father extended an arm. "Gavin and I were just talking about what a wonderful evening this was. And I have you to thank for forcing me to buy a ticket." He turned to Gavin. "Bree has a soft spot for animals."

Bree managed a polite smile.

"It was a great pleasure to meet you, Bree." Gavin's eyes met hers.

Instantly a flare of heat rushed to her face and her heart began to pound like a jackhammer. "Likewise," she stammered.

"Are you free on Friday? The firm is having a cocktail party at the Rosa Lounge to celebrate a new campaign. I'd love you to come."

Bree's mind spun. Friday night? That was a serious dating night. And he wanted her to meet all his business associates? Her mouth dried.

"Uh, sure. That would be nice." She blinked rapidly.

"I'll pick you up at your house, if that's okay."

"That would be great." She smiled as calmly as she could. "I'll see you then."

"See you later, darling." Her father shot her a tight smile. "I have some friends to catch up with."

"Sure, I'll get a cab."

Gavin stepped toward her. "I'll drive you home. Then I'll know where to come find you on Friday."

He summoned a porter to tell valet parking before Bree could protest.

She inhaled deeply, took his offered arm and walked outside. The light mist of rain that had followed her to the Four Seasons earlier had evaporated, leaving a clear moonlit night that illuminated the sturdy bank buildings across Market Street and gave them the grandeur of real Roman temples. Stars glimmered overhead as Gavin helped her into the passenger seat of his low-slung sports car.

They chatted about the new Louise Bourgeois exhibit at the Modern on the short drive home. Gavin admitted he went often to keep on top of emerging trends so he could impress clients. He was embarrassingly gorgeous *and* he knew about art?

She leaped out of the car in front of her house, heart pounding. Would he try to kiss her?

Impossible.

Or was it?

Terror streaked along her veins as he rounded the car toward her. He took her hand, which was sweating slightly. A shiver of heat shot right up her arm.

"Good night, Bree." He clasped her hand in both of his, warm and firm. Their gazes held and her lips quivered with a mix of anticipation and apprehension.

Then he tilted his head. "I'll pick you up at seven on Friday, if that's okay."

"Perfect. See you then." She flashed a smile, then turned and scurried for the door.

Once inside she literally collapsed against it. And a big, wide, goofy smile spread across her face.

She had a Friday-night date with the most handsome man in San Francisco.

And if she weren't so freaked out, she'd be pretty darn thrilled about it.

Two

"Gavin, sweetie, how are you?" Marissa Curtis assaulted him as he entered the Rosa Lounge with Bree on his arm. She wrapped her skinny arms around him and kissed him on both cheeks, overwhelming him with that eye-watering fragrance she always wore. "I've missed you this week. Were you in Cannes?"

"Yes. Had some meetings." He'd had a really good time at the film festival, and it had given him a chance to plan his campaign to win Bree Kincannon, who stood rather patiently beside him.

"Marissa, this is Bree. Bree, Marissa."

"Oh, lovely to meet you." The blonde smiled, revealing frighteningly white teeth. "Are you Gavin's sister?"

Gavin exploded into a laugh. "My sister? I don't even have a sister."

"Oh." Marissa tipped her silly head to the side, so her silky hair cascaded artfully over her shoulder. "I just thought…" She looked mischievously at Bree.

"That Bree and I look so alike we must be twins?" Gavin wrapped his arm around Bree. She was stiff as a board.

Catty Marissa was no doubt trying to imply that Bree couldn't possibly be his date. After all, she wasn't built like a twig and dressed in Prada.

"Bree's my date."

"Oh." Marissa's grimace widened. "How charming." She widened her eyes rudely. "Must dash. I see Jake. He said he'd bring me something nice back from Cannes."

Gavin turned to Bree. "Don't mind her. She's just insane."

Bree's sweet smile reappeared, giving him a warm feeling in his chest. He liked her smile.

"And you know, we do kind of look alike." He rubbed her shoulder. "We've both got dark hair and gray eyes. Or wait, are yours green?" On closer inspection, the irises hiding behind her metal-framed glasses looked like pale jade. "I couldn't see you properly the other night. It was so dark at the gala." They were close enough for him to enjoy her scent—subtle and fresh, like the rest of her.

"They're probably more gray than green." Bree shrugged. "Doesn't make much difference to me. I just use them for looking out of."

"And taking pictures. I looked up your Black Book photos. Those were some amazing portraits."

"Interesting faces." She smiled shyly, her lips rosy and inviting. "Made my job easy."

"Who were they?" Her crisp black-and-white image of the older couple, standing outside on a city street, their bold, cheerful countenances sunlit and their happy union obvious, rather haunted him since he'd seen it. Something about the photo made it hard to forget.

"I don't even know. Isn't that embarrassing? I'll be exposed as a fraud." She bit her lip. "They were just standing there outside the library, waiting for someone, I think. I asked if I could take their picture."

"I'd never guess you hadn't known them for decades."

"That's what everyone says." She shrugged. "It's a little weird, I guess."

"It's art." He grinned. She was starting to relax. Good. "Hey, Elle. Come meet Bree." He beckoned to Brock Maddox's assistant. The slim brunette pushed past two art directors to join them. "Bree's a photographer."

"Are you really?"

"Award winning," pronounced Gavin. "Can I leave Bree in your capable hands for a moment, Elle? I need to chat with Brock."

"Sure. First we'll get her a drink. Follow me

to the bar." Elle led Bree off into the thickening crowd.

Gavin scanned the room for Brock. He'd had a great meeting in Cannes with a hot new Czech director who might be willing to shoot a campaign for the right price. Gavin wasn't sure Brock would go for Tomas Kozinski's "right price," but it was worth a try. He had a unique, hand-held style that made even the scenery come alive.

"Hey, Gavin, how's it going? Still getting cozy with the Rialto yacht people?" Logan Emerson materialized in front of him, wine glass raised.

Irritation prickled Gavin's neck. "Trying to."

"That account would be a really big score. I can already see those Rialtos sailing under the Golden Gate Bridge at halftime on Super Bowl night."

"That might be a tad predictable."

"I guess that's why I'm an account exec and not a copywriter." Logan chuckled and slapped him on the back.

Gavin inhaled. Something about this guy really bothered him, and it wasn't just his bad jokes. Logan Emerson had only been at the company a few weeks, but already he seemed to be underfoot all day long: in every meeting; loitering by the espresso machine; he even wandered into the damned men's room whenever Gavin entered. Sometimes, like now, he'd be all smiles and jollities, but most of the time he just stood there. Watching.

Maybe he was trying to soak up the Maddox modus operandi so he could beat the other account executives at their own game. Which wasn't such a bad thing. At least then Gavin wouldn't feel too bad about leaving Brock in the lurch when he quit to start his own company.

Hopefully soon.

He cast his eyes around the room and was relieved and pleased to see Bree, wine glass in hand, chatting with Elle.

So far, so good.

"Actually my undergrad major was English." Bree took a sip from her delicate glass. Elle had snagged some white wine, then ushered her into a relatively quiet corner of the sleek bar, where they could talk. Bree felt a bit intimidated by her at first. Elle was so polished and put together in a tailored suit that showed off her slim figure. Her brown hair was sleek as sable and her blue eyes shone with intelligence and good humor.

After a few minutes, though, she started to relax, answering questions that Elle seemed to have asked with genuine interest. "At the time I thought I might even pursue a PhD in English, but I took some time off to travel and changed my mind. Flaky, I guess."

Elle smiled. "Not flaky, thoughtful. A lot of people rush ahead with some big plan they've had in their mind for years, and end up painted into a corner doing something that isn't their passion. I have to admit, I've always been mad about photography. I took a lot of classes in high school and college, but I guess I've never been daring enough to try to publish or exhibit my pictures. What got you started in photography?"

"I'm embarrassed to admit this, but it was a

total accident. My dad gave me a camera for my birthday four years ago. I actually think a client gave it to him as a gift, as he doesn't know anything about them, but it was a top of the line Nikon, with a set of extra lenses. The kind of thing even a professional photographer would salivate over. I started fooling around with it—taking pictures of old oak trees in the park, and interesting buildings around Russian Hill and the Marina District."

Elle nodded, her blue eyes alight with interest. Bree felt a warm connection to her, even though they'd just met.

"One day I was taking a picture of St. Francis of Assisi on Vallejo Street."

"Oh, yes. The one with all the doorways."

"You know how that woman in the blue coat is often there?"

"Feeding the pigeons. Yes, totally!" Elle smiled.

"Something about her intrigued me. She has such a sense of purpose. I have no idea why she's there and I'd never ask. I'm far too shy."

She pushed a stray hair off her cheek. Somehow Elle had put her so at ease that she didn't feel shy at all. "But I wanted to see if I could take a picture of that quiet dignity she exudes."

"What did you say?"

"I just asked if I could take her picture." Bree grinned. "I know now that I should have offered her two dollars and a model release form, but I was clueless at the time."

"And she said yes."

Bree nodded. "So I took the picture. Took only a few seconds—just her, standing there in front of the smallest door, her coat buttoned up to her neck like always, with that flock of pigeons at her feet. The shots came out pretty well, so I printed one and entered it in a small show at the local library. My image won, and people started making a fuss, so I figured I'd keep snapping away."

"I'd love to see that picture."

"You're welcome to come up to my studio any time."

"Really?" Elle's eyes lit up. "I'd love to! I've never been in a real photographer's studio."

"Oh, I wouldn't call it that." Bree blushed. "But it does have a lovely view out over the rooftops. I'm around tomorrow, if you'd like to come by."

"Can I? I don't have to be anywhere until five. It would be so nice to see some photographs that aren't glossy product shots for a change." She winked conspiratorially. "If I come in the morning, I could bring some pastries and coffee from Stella's."

"You're on. I can never say no to their bear claws. The address is 200 Talbot Street. The limestone behemoth with the wrought-iron gates. If you come around the right-hand side there's a separate entrance up to my studio."

"Planning a secret tryst?" Gavin's deep voice made her spin around. His gray eyes looked at her with amusement.

"Absolutely." Elle grinned. "I want to see Bree's work before she gets too famous to talk to me. Did you know she's been asked to shoot a portrait for *San Francisco Magazine?*"

"Is that true?" Gavin tilted his head.

"It is." Bree blushed again, wishing she were actually as cool as everyone seemed to think she was. "I'm shooting Robert Pattison. They had a tough time deciding between Annie Leibowitz and me. I suspect I was cheaper." Gavin's dimples appeared. "They just called me out of the blue. Saw my pictures in Black Book."

"That's awesome." Gavin's rich voice rang with admiration. "I'd like to see your photos, too."

"Form a line, form a line," joked Elle, raising her glass. "But seriously, Robert Pattison? I wish I was a jet-setting photographer and not a lowly administrative assistant." She did a mock pout.

Bree very much doubted that Elle was just a "lowly administrative assistant." She waved and chatted with everyone as if she was the owner of the company, not the owner's right-hand woman.

"Hang tough, Cinderella. You'll get to go to the ball one day. But in the meantime, you'd better find your boss. I haven't seen him anywhere."

"I'll go track him down. Nice to meet you, Bree, and I'll see you tomorrow."

Elle marched smartly off into the crowd.

"Brock has been a bit distracted lately." Gavin leaned in until his delicious masculine scent stole over her. "A lot going on."

The clang of a spoon hitting a glass snagged their attention.

Bree turned to see a gray-haired man in a conservative suit, wreathed in smiles. Amazingly, the entire room fell silent.

"It's our oldest client," murmured Gavin. "Walter Prentice. We're here to celebrate the launch of a new campaign for his company planned by Celia, one of our account execs. It's going really well."

"It's a great pleasure to spend an evening with the most impressive creative talent in the entire United States." The older man's voice carried through the crowded space. "In the years my company has worked with Maddox Communications, I've been pleased to get to know many of you as personal friends. I've just learned that Flynn Maddox and his lovely wife, Renee, are expecting their first baby. I'd like you to join with me in celebrating their new family with a champagne toast."

Already waiters carried trays full of champagne glasses around the room.

"Flynn is Brock Maddox's younger brother. He got back together with his wife recently after a long separation." Gavin's warm breath tickled her ear.

"How lovely." Bree smiled and accepted a sparkling glass of bubbly. "And very sweet of your client to make a fuss."

"He's a nice guy. Very family oriented. Been married to his wife, Angela, for forty years."

"Impressive. Nearly all my dad's friends are divorced. Some of them several times."

"That's a shame." Gavin sipped his champagne. "Marriage should be for life—otherwise what's the point?"

His earnest gaze met hers—and made her gulp champagne too fast. "I'm sure you're right. But I've never been married, so I have no idea what it's really like." Her words came out a bit rushed. It was downright freaky to be discussing marriage on a first date, let alone a first date with a man like Gavin Spencer.

"Me, either." He grinned, boyish and charming. "But I hope that when I do tie the knot, it will be the kind of marriage I'll toast with champagne forty years later."

Bree tugged her eyes away. Okay, she must be dreaming. This couldn't possibly be real. There was no such thing as a gorgeous, dashing and successful man who wanted to stay married to one woman for life.

Was there?

Walter Prentice raised his filled champagne glass. "A toast to the happy couple! May their family be blessed with many years of happiness, and not too many sleepless nights." He grinned.

"My own children have brought me so much joy. I know that Flynn and Renee will be fantastic parents."

He looked down, then directly at a tall, black-haired man, who Bree guessed might be Flynn. "You know our company slogan—family is everything. Well, it's not just a slogan, it's a way of life." He raised his glass.

The room buzzed with cheers. "Oh, my gosh, that really is their slogan, isn't it?" Bree laughed. "I've seen their ads on TV."

Gavin's gray eyes twinkled. "I guess sometimes believing your own publicity isn't such a bad thing. Hey, there's Brock. Come meet the big boss."

Bree's eyes widened as he slid his fingers to the small of her back to guide her across the room, claiming her as his date in front of everyone—friends, coworkers, clients. Almost as if he was showing her off.

She fought the urge to pinch herself. Any

minute now she'd wake up in her own bed, with Faith and Ali stretched, purring, on the duvet next to her. But until then she'd better keep a smile on her face.

Never a morning person, Bree had barely managed to drag herself out of bed by the time Elle showed up at her door. She and Gavin had stayed at the party until nearly 1 a.m. Once again, he'd dropped her home without dropping a hint about coming in.

And without trying to kiss her.

"Hey, Bree!" Elle kissed her on the cheek like they were old friends. "I brought your bear claw and some coffee. I bet you need it after last night. Gavin must have introduced you to everyone in the room." She handed Bree a to-go cup full of steaming coffee.

"He may have even introduced me to some of them twice. It was all a blur after about ten o'clock. Come in." She ushered Elle into the bright room. Ornate Victorian paned glass covered one wall and part of the sloped ceiling, creating the bright studio light that gave the space its name.

"Oh, my lord, look at the view." Elle put the paper bakery bag on the small dining table and moved to the window. "I bet on a clear day you can see Japan from here."

"Almost." Bree grinned. "I do love watching boats in the bay."

"I guess you'll miss the view when you move in with Gavin." Elle lifted a brow.

Bree froze. "What? There's nothing going on between Gavin and me. I only just met him."

"Really?" Elle's eyes widened. "I got the definite impression that you two were a serious item."

"He was being very…solicitous, but I only met him the night before."

"You're kidding me." Elle's eyes narrowed. "I know you and I only just met, so I shouldn't even ask this, but you've kissed, right?"

"Not even a peck." A prickle of embarrassment ran over her. If she were cute like Elle, he probably would have tried. "I think he's just being friendly."

"But he kept putting his arm around you." Elle cocked her head. "That's not the kind of thing you do with a friend. Nope. He's definitely after you. Probably just taking it slow."

Bree shrugged, hoping the heat in her face didn't show. "Let me get some plates."

They chatted about the house and the neighborhood while they ate their pastries and sipped the strong coffee. After they ate, Bree showed Elle some of her photos.

"You have an amazing eye. In each picture there's something of the essence of the individual. I know how hard that is to capture. I can't take a decent portrait to save my life. I'm lucky if their eyes are open."

"I wish I could offer some tips, but I'm afraid I'm not sure how I do it."

"Genius. Talent. All those things I don't have as a photographer." Elle smiled. "It's not hard to see why Gavin's crazy about you."

"Oh, stop! First of all, he's not crazy about me. Second of all, he hasn't seen my photos."

"Yes, he has. He was showing everyone the Black Book in the office on Friday."

"Was he really?" Bree bit her lip.

"One word. Besotted." Elle crossed her arms. "A man in love. Sometimes it happens that fast."

"Oh, come on. What could Gavin possibly see in me? I'm definitely not the type men fall head over heels for."

"What makes you say that?"

"Well, let's see. My hair has a mind of its own, which changes with the barometric pressure. I need to lose weight. And the only famous person I bear a resemblance to is one Duncan Kincannon, Tenth Laird of Aislin. You can see him halfway down the stairs in the main hall, wrapped in a gilt frame."

Elle giggled. "I bet Gavin loves your sense of humor."

"That's about all there is to love."

"What nonsense! Though…" She tipped her head to one side and pressed a figure to her lips. "If you don't mind my saying so…I can see a little room for improvement."

Bree cringed inside her baggy college sweatshirt. "More than a little room, I'm afraid."

"You're lovely as you are, but you could be lovelier. I spent a summer working at a froufrou spa in Santa Barbara. I learned all kinds of brilliant tricks there."

"Like what?"

"Your hair. It's curly, right?"

"I think frizzy is a better description."

"No, seriously, will you take it down for a sec?"

Bree pulled the ponytail band from her hair with shaky fingers. The heavy mass fell— frizzily—over her shoulders.

"Oh, yes. You've got lovely ringlets in there. We just have to set them free."

"How do you do that?"

Elle smiled mysteriously. "We need to gather a few tools."

* * *

It was nearly four in the afternoon by the time Elle was satisfied with her work. They'd spent an hour in the sun while Elle filed and polished Bree's nails, and they waited for artfully applied lemon juice to scorch highlights into Bree's hair.

Next, Elle conditioned her hair. She'd rinsed, then applied yet more conditioner—gloppy handfuls of it—and made Bree swear she'd never let her hair dry without conditioner on it again.

While Bree dripped conditioner onto the wood floors, Elle rifled through her wardrobe, tut-tutting and holding items up to Bree's complexion. In despair, she marched Bree—hair still damp—out the door and down to Union Street, where she encouraged her to try on, and ultimately buy, three very expensive new bras and several mix-and-match pieces from a trendy boutique. Elle made the whole thing so enjoyable, Bree felt as if they were BFFs out for an adventure rather than two women who'd only met the night before.

Once coordinating shoes were found, they hurried back to the apartment where Elle applied a loose powder all over her face, "to brighten you up a bit," as she said. She brushed light blush over Bree's cheekbones, and smudged gray-green shadow around her eyes. A touch of rose-pink lipstick gave a subtle punch to her color, without making her look like a clown.

"Your hair's finally dry." Elle arranged it about her shoulders. "Why don't you look in the mirror?"

Half afraid of what she'd see, Bree made her way across the studio—no small feat in the heeled ankle boots Elle had talked her into.

A long mirror hung behind the bathroom door, and she inhaled as she pulled it open.

She squinted for a moment, looking the image up and down. Then she laughed aloud. "Who is that woman in my mirror?"

"It's you, babe."

"Not possible. This woman is trim and elegant, and has silky ringlets with blond highlights."

"It's all you. Standing up straight is a big part of it. Tall girls like you often stoop because you're afraid to stand out. If you do those yoga poses I showed you just once a day, you'll really see a difference in your posture."

"It never would have occurred to me that clothes which fit could make me look thinner!"

"You have a gorgeous, curvy figure and you should show it off."

"Who knew?" Bree grinned at her reflection. "And I swear on my life, I'll never let my hair dry without conditioner again."

"That's my girl. So, when are you seeing Gavin next?"

Three

Gavin called on Sunday and invited Bree to a gallery opening on Tuesday night. A photography show. Said he wanted her opinion of the artist's work.

Naturally, she said yes.

For the opening she chose a wrap dress in a dark eggplant color that was subtle and dramatic at the same time. The cut flattered her hourglass figure—who knew she had one?—and made an asset of her height. For the first time in years, she wore heels, which probably made her about five foot eleven. She'd bravely "washed" her hair using only conditioner and it had come out shockingly well—a mass of shiny ringlets. As she sparingly applied some of the subtle makeup Elle had left for her, she wondered how Gavin would react.

At seven o'clock on the dot she heard a knock on the private door to her studio.

Heart pounding, she crossed the slippery wood floor as gracefully as possible in her heels and pulled it open.

"Hi, Br—" Gavin's mouth fell open.

"Hey, Gavin." She smiled. "How was work today?"

"Great. It was really good." He blinked, and peered at her curiously. "You look different."

"Just a little." She shrugged and turned into the loft. Part of her wanted to laugh out loud. "New dress."

"It looks stunning on you." His voice was deeper than usual. He looked devastating himself, in dark pants and a white shirt with a barely visible gray stripe.

"Thanks. Let me get my bag." She slung

the small beaded vintage purse, which used to belong to her mom, over her shoulder. "I'm looking forward to the exhibit."

"Me, too." She turned to see him staring at her, a furrow between his brows.

"Something wrong?"

"Oh, no." He blinked. "No, nothing at all." He glanced lower, taking in the soft drape of her new dress over her hips. Her skin hummed under his hungry gaze.

He does find me attractive.

The feeling was utterly new, a strange and surprising thrill. She pulled her shoulders back, trying to maintain the posture Elle had showed her, and to hide the fact that her pulse was still pounding and her palms sweating, despite her composed appearance.

Gavin cleared his throat. "My car's downstairs."

They walked into the Razor gallery arm in arm. She was only a couple of inches shorter than him in her new heels. Eyes, once again, turned to stare. But this time they weren't glares of female indignation that she—lowly and insignificant plain Jane—was on Gavin's arm.

No, this time the men were looking, too.

Bree tossed her curls behind her shoulders as she accepted a glass of white wine. "Shall we look at the images?"

Even her voice sounded sultrier, as if overnight she'd morphed into a more sophisticated version of herself.

They looked closely at the photographs. Large digital prints of people, mostly at parties and nightclubs, the colors highly saturated and intoxicating. "I can almost hear the music," she said, looking at a couple entwined on a dance floor, perspiration gleaming on their barely clad bodies.

"That's why I like Doug's images. They invoke the other senses. I'm hoping he'll do a vodka campaign I have in mind. It's hard to make a flat piece of paper say 'drink me,' but I think this guy could pull it off." He pointed the artist out to Bree—a short, skinny guy with numerous piercings, a goatee and an air of manic enthusiasm.

"Now, he looks like an artist," she whispered. "Maybe I need to pierce my nose. What do you think?" She tilted her head, fighting the urge to grin.

"Definitely not. Your nose is absolutely perfect already." Gavin's warm gray gaze rested on her face. Her skin sizzled slightly under the heat of his admiration. "Your eyes are green."

"Yes." She blushed. "I got contacts." Elle had talked her into trying tinted ones.

"They're cute. And I can see you better without glasses in the way."

"Aren't we here to look at art? I'm starting to feel self-conscious."

Though she had to admit it was a good feeling to be admired. When Gavin went to get them fresh glasses of wine, a tall man with spiky blond hair approached her and made small talk about the images.

The look on Gavin's face when he returned was priceless.

He had to get Bree out of here.

Gavin tried not to scowl at the punk who'd

horned in on her while he turned his back for a moment. He recognized the guy, a Finnish video editor with a tinny laugh. They'd worked together on a storyboard. "Hey, Lars. How's it going?"

"Good, Gavin. Good." He turned his gel-crusted head back to Bree. "So you're a photographer, too?"

"Yes." Bree smiled sweetly. Gavin hadn't noticed how full and lush her lips were before. Lust mingled with irritation in his veins. "Well, kind of. I haven't actually done a professional shoot yet."

"Bree and I were just heading out to dinner." His statement was more of a growl than he'd intended.

Every man in the room was looking at her. And who could blame them? The richly colored dress draped her curves in a way that should be illegal. In her heels she was probably the tallest women in the room, and with the regal tilt of her head and her cascade of shiny gold-tipped curls, she shone like a goddess.

"I'd love to take a quick peek at the images in the next room. Lars was just telling me about them. They're portraits of the artist's friends."

Gavin decided he'd like to tell Lars a thing or two. But he resisted the primal urges surging in his blood. "Sure, let's go look."

He slid his arm through Bree's, claiming her, and guided her across the floor. He couldn't resist scowling at one dark-haired charmer who shot Bree a look so flirtatious it was downright tacky.

"Oh, look at this sweet couple," she exclaimed. He peered into a small square-framed image. A pair of teenage lovers were wrapped in each other on a park bench.

Gavin could readily imagine being in such a clinch with Bree. Her lush curves called out to him, urging his palms to explore their hills and valleys.

Arousal surged through him, and he tugged his gaze from Bree's breathtaking cleavage back to the artwork at hand. "Very nice," he murmured.

She tossed her cascade of curls behind her shoulder. He could almost swear her hair looked totally different last time he'd seen her. It had been tied back—maybe that was it.

It wasn't just the hair. Something was very different about Bree. She'd been pretty in a quiet and unassuming way when they'd met. Now she was undeniably a knockout. Even the way she carried herself seemed altered. Before, her shoulders were rounded, apologetic. Now she threw them back proudly.

Her stiff evening gown had concealed her body at the gala. This drapey number revealed it in tantalizing detail—her backside was a work of art all by itself. His fingers itched to pull at the bow tied her waist and unwrap the delicious present in front of him. "Are you hungry?"

Because I know I am. And not for food.

And her father was going to give him a million dollars to marry her? He'd approached the renowned venture capitalist to discuss an investment in his proposed business, and Kincannon had shocked him with his own proposal: one million dollars and his still-unwed daughter. Gavin's first instinct had been to refuse, but he agreed to meet her. Now, his good fortune seemed almost unbelievable. And he certainly didn't want to blow it by letting some wiseass muscle in on his prize.

"Uh, sure. What did you have in mind?" She blinked, those rich green eyes shining in a way they hadn't behind her glasses. "There's a good Thai place about a block away."

"Perfect. Let's go." He wrapped his arm firmly around her waist as they moved back to the main gallery. No way would he let another guy get his hooks into Bree Kincannon.

He shot a warning stare around the room. Hands off. She's mine.

Her hips shifted from side to side under his arm, stirring heat in his groin. His pursuit of Bree was fast morphing from a business proposition into a personal quest. He couldn't remember the last time he'd been so aroused by a woman.

At the restaurant he requested a quiet table in

the back room—a gold spangled festival of Thai kitsch—where they could talk undisturbed. He admired the rear view as he helped Bree into her chair.

She shook out her napkin. "The pad thai's really good."

"I'll get that then." He didn't feel like reading the menu. He was far more interested in looking at her. A tiny silver heart hung from a fine chain around her neck, dancing dangerously near the enticing cleft between her breasts.

Now all he had to do was convince Bree he should be her future husband.

He poured some San Pellegrino into her glass. "Have you always lived in San Francisco?"

"We used to spend summers in Napa Valley when I was little, before my mom died, but other than that, yes. I've lived in the same house in Russian Hill since I was a baby."

"That's a lovely neighborhood."

"I suspect that's what my ancestors said when they built the house a hundred years ago. It's lasted through several earthquakes and is big enough for me to share with my father without us driving each other nuts, so I'm very fond of it."

"Is it strange still living at home with your dad?"

"I'm used to it, so it's not at all strange to me. I'm sure some people think it's a bit pathetic and that I should strike out on my own." She sipped her water. "I suppose I will someday. When the moment is right."

Phew. Gavin didn't much fancy sharing a house with the old man. Especially since Elliott Kincannon was about to become his benefactor.

"Does your family live in San Francisco?" Her innocent question tugged him back to the present.

"San Diego, but I moved away from home when I was seventeen and never looked back. My dad wanted me to follow family tradition and join the military. He was furious when I applied to UCLA and got a full scholarship to study marketing. We had a big blowup and I left that night."

"How awful! Did you patch things up?"

"It took about four years for him to give up his dreams of seeing me in a dress uniform covered in medals, but he's happy that I'm successful doing something I like."

"That's all that matters, really, isn't it? My dad couldn't understand why I kept taking jobs at nonprofit organizations that paid me less than my age. I enjoyed the work and was glad to help. And since I already had a nice place to live, I didn't need to rake in big bucks."

"You're lucky. I had a tough time right out of school. I was ready to take on the world and become CEO of General Electric, and my boss kept wanting me to file his papers and answer his phone instead."

Bree laughed. "Trust me, it's not much different at a nonprofit. Though there are less people so you have to pitch in more. I think it's good to start at the bottom—then you get a chance to watch how other people do things."

"And learn from their mistakes."

"That, too." Her bright smile flashed again, sending a charge of excitement through him. "Do you like working for Maddox Communications?"

"Sure. It's one of the top agencies on the West Coast. We have some of the biggest clients in America."

She cocked her head slightly. "Hmm, those are awfully generic reasons to like a place."

"I like Brock and Flynn Maddox, too. They inherited the family business from their dad, but they've done a lot with it."

Was it wise to tell her he wanted to strike out on his own? Probably not. Then she might start wondering if he was more interested in her funds than in her.

They gave their orders to the waiter, who quickly returned with their beers.

"I suspect my dad is disappointed that I don't want to be a venture capitalist." Bree raised her brows. "He can't understand why anyone would do something unless there's a profit involved."

"Crazy." Gavin managed to keep a straight face.

"I swear, I think the reason he never married again is that he couldn't find anyone richer than himself to marry!"

Bree laughed, and Gavin forced himself to join in. He had to make sure she *never* found out about her dad's proposition. "What do you think is a good reason to get married?" He poured some beer into her glass.

Bree looked up, as if studying the patterned ceiling for an answer. "Love, I suppose. What other reason could there be?"

His stomach clenched slightly. "Have you ever been in love?"

"Not since third grade. Randy Plimpton broke my heart so badly when he sat with Jessica Slade at the end-of-year picnic that I never recovered." A mischievous sparkle lit her eyes.

"That sounds devastating. I can see how you'd never trust your heart to a man again."

"That's how I felt. I guess that must explain

why I've never even had a real boyfriend." Her cheeks colored slightly.

"That Randy has a lot to answer for. On the other hand, if you'd had a serious boyfriend you might have married him. Then you wouldn't be sitting here sipping Thai beer with me." He raised his glass.

"I guess there's a good side to everything." Bree clinked her glass against his and took a sip. Her adorable nose wrinkled. "I don't drink much, either. I've led a very dull life, really."

"Perhaps that's all about to change."

Bree's eyes widened. "Do you think?"

"I do. I have a funny feeling about it." He cocked his head and let his gaze drift over her face. Her lips parted slightly, moist, as if they'd like to be kissed.

Which hopefully they would be in the very near future.

Bree took a tentative sip of the golden liquid, then blinked as she swallowed it down. "You know what? I'm ready for change. I'm tired of sitting on the sidelines of life. I'm ready to get out and enjoy it more."

Their pad thai arrived, steaming and fragrant with basil. They ate in silence for a few moments. Then Gavin decided to head deeper into dangerous territory.

"I've had girlfriends before, but never one that I thought was 'the one.'"

"I wonder how it's different. If you just *know* a person is the one you'll spend the rest of your life with." Her smooth brow wrinkled slightly. "That must be an amazing feeling."

"I hear it happens fast."

Her brows rose. "Love at first sight?"

"Something like that. The person just clicks with you."

Bree inhaled deeply, which drew his gaze to her bosom. Gavin's arousal thickened at the sight of her full breasts under the clingy dress.

She looked up at him, eyes soft. "I hope I'll find that one day. You know, someone I can feel totally comfortable with."

Maybe you already have.

Gavin tilted his head. "It could be the kind of thing that sneaks up on you as you get to know the person."

"You mean like one minute they're a friend and the next…you can't keep your hands off them?" She giggled.

"I'm sure that happens to people all the time." Her laugh tickled something deep inside him. "Probably just when they least expect it."

Gavin dropped Bree home and said goodbye with a restrained peck on the cheek. She didn't invite him in, though she looked as if she wanted to. He wanted to keep things slow and steady, rather than rush in too hot and heavy and possibly scare her off.

For their next date, he invited her to a jazz concert at the Palace of Fine Arts. For dinner he brought a carefully packed picnic from the gourmet store near his apartment, and a bottle of champagne. Bree, resplendent in a midnight blue dress and sparkly silver earrings, blushed with delight as he spread a blanket under a huge shade tree on the grounds and unpacked the food. The weather was warm and calm.

"I've always wanted to come for a picnic here," she exclaimed. "It's got to be one of the most romantic spots in the city."

He looked up from the feast he was unpacking. "Tonight seemed like the perfect opportunity."

"Look at the way the sunset lights up the lagoon." The expanse of water shimmered like liquid gold. Around them other couples and groups laughed and dined and took in the beauty of the spring evening. "The city has so many interesting places. You could live here for decades and never visit them all.

"And what a shame that would be." Bree unwrapped a lacquer box filled with stuffed grape leaves. "Ooh, one of my favorites. I swear the Kincannons must have Greek ancestry somewhere. We're all crazy about Greek food."

"You fit right in with the architecture then. Or is this Roman?" He glanced up at the heavily ornamented Corinthian style columns that adorned the massive buildings nestled around the lake.

Bree laughed. "They were built in 1915 for the World's Fair here in San Francisco. I'd call them World's Fair Classical. I love how 'over the top' they are. The original buildings were made of paper, and only meant to last a year. They proved pretty sturdy and by the time they started to fall down decades later, everyone was so attached to the place that they decided to rebuild it permanently."

The fading sun gleamed in her curls, lighting up the gold highlights. Her skin shone, cheeks still pink with excitement. He wanted to kiss her right now....

But he resisted. "How do you know so much about everything?"

"Just curious, I guess. And I have lived here my whole life."

"Do you plan to spend the rest of your life here?" He wasn't entirely sure why he asked. Did he want to find out if she had a life plan already mapped out, and if so, if she'd be happy to reconfigure it for him?

She frowned slightly, then smiled. "I don't know. I guess it all depends on where life takes me."

"As a photographer you can work any-where."

She laughed. "I still don't think of myself as a photographer. I've only been offered one profes-sional assignment so far. I haven't even done it yet. What if it's a disaster?"

"It will be fantastic. Is this the one for *San Francisco Magazine?*"

"Yes. It's next week. Robert Pattinson, for crying out loud! I'm paralyzed with nerves."

"You move very well for someone with paralysis." He offered her a dish of stuffed olives, and she smiled and took one. "Do you have to fly to New York for the shoot?"

"No, he's coming here for a movie premiere. At least if everything goes as planned. Maybe he'll cancel at the last minute." She tucked a curl nervously behind her ear and bit her lip.

"He won't cancel. He's a professional. And you'll do an amazing job. Just think, soon your picture will be pirated all over the internet."

"Oh, stop! I just hope I don't annoy him, or drop my camera or something. It's got to be film, not digital. I think that's one of the reasons they asked me."

"They asked you because you're amazingly talented and they know everyone will be talking about the pictures. Just relax and try to enjoy it." He stroked her arm. Her dress was silky soft jersey material that draped lusciously over her curves. Heat flared in his groin and he had to resist the urge to let his hand trail over more of her delicious body.

All in good time, he promised himself. He needed at least a few dates with her under his belt before he made any kind of…move. Though the temptation to make one right now was killing him.

Especially when she shifted, and the fabric of her dress pulled tight for a moment over her tantalizing breasts.

Ouch. His pants suddenly felt tight.

Her eyes sparkled as she sipped her champagne. "I'm excited about the concert. I've been going to jazz concerts regularly over the past year. I'm really starting to get the music."

He smiled. "Then you can teach me. All I do is enjoy it."

"That works, too. It's so nice to meet someone who likes doing so many of the things I enjoy."

"I love walking around with you. You know so much of the city."

Her eyes brightened. "I'd be happy to roam around more of it with you."

He offered her some marinated chicken in a pita and she put it on her plate. "Where do you recommend?"

"How about the Marina? Or the Painted Ladies—the Victorian houses, of course, not the hookers—near the park? Alcatraz is pretty wild. Have you ever been there?"

"No, and now I can't wait to go to each and every one of them."

* * *

Why hadn't he kissed her yet? Bree examined her carefully made up face in the mirror. Gavin was due any minute—again. They'd seen each other every other day for the past two weeks, walked nearly a hundred miles around the city, eaten countless meals and even—gasp!—held hands.

But not a single kiss on the lips. He brushed her cheek lightly with his lips when they said goodbye, but that was it.

Maybe he wasn't attracted to her, after all?

She should be exhilarated after her shoot. Despite a late start, everything had gone smoothly and the proofs were to die for. The star was every bit as charming and polite as she'd imagined, and she'd managed not to blush and stammer like a teenager in his presence. She even showed him her portfolio so he'd have some idea of who the heck was taking his picture, and he'd asked all kinds of questions and seemed genuinely enthusiastic about her work.

She should be over the moon. Her first

professional assignment was safely under her belt and she had another date with the most gorgeous man in San Francisco.

So why did she feel so…uneasy?

Gavin *seemed* to be interested. Something twinkled in his eyes when he looked at her, and she'd caught him sneaking glances at her cleavage, which had been on display more over the last couple of weeks than ever in her life.

He laughed at her jokes and appeared intrigued by all the odd anecdotes she'd picked up over the years. At one point, in the quiet gloom of an abandoned Alcatraz cell, she could almost swear he was going to step forward and kiss her. Tension hummed in the air like whispered voices of the people who'd been captive there. Her skin tingled at his nearness and she hoped with bated breath that he'd reach out to her.

But he didn't. And once again, after the ferry ride back, he said goodbye by pressing his lips gently to her cheek.

Good old Bree. Not really the kissable type. Perhaps he saw her more as a friend. Or a sister, even, as that catty woman at his office party had suggested.

A sharp knock on the door tugged her back to the present. Her heart pounded under her latest clothing purchase, a stylish blouse with fine green and gray stripes. She added an extra hint of gloss to her lips for luck. Maybe he'd notice them and want to put his own lips on them tonight. If not, she might have to take matters into her own hands.

As if she had the nerve for that.

She pulled open the door and, as usual, her lungs squeezed with excitement and a big goofy grin pulled at her lips. "Hi, Gavin."

"Hi, Bree." The chaste cheek kiss he gave her still made her knees weak. How could a man smell so good after a long day at the office? Like wind and sea air and adventure. He'd changed into a pale blue shirt and faded jeans that hugged his thighs like a lover. "How do you feel about a walk to the Coit Tower on Telegraph Hill?"

"Great." Yeah, just great. The most popular

proposal spot in the city and she was going to go there and maybe hold hands if she got lucky.

Unless…

She swallowed hard. No. Gavin Spencer was not going to propose to her tonight. This was the twenty-first century, not the eighteenth. A man did not ask a woman to marry him after accompanying her on a few bracing walks.

"There's a neat little Italian restaurant nearby, too, so we could grab some dinner."

"Sounds lovely." Her reply came out sounding a bit forced.

Gavin cocked his head. "Are you sure? Because we don't have to go if you don't want to."

"No, really, I'd love to." She reached down to grab her bag.

"And I was thinking that afterward, if you'd like, you could come back to my place for a nightcap."

"Oh. Sure, that would be great." Suddenly she was all breathless excitement. Her cheeks heated. He surely wouldn't ask her back to his place unless he intended to…

Butterflies unfurled in her stomach. What exactly did he have in mind? Possibly quite a bit more than a kiss.

"Let's go." He held out his hand and she took it. The door slammed behind her with a resounding thud.

They walked briskly through the streets to Telegraph Hill, where the pale spire of the tower rose above the surrounding houses. The climb up the hill toward the tower left Bree panting. "I can't believe you haven't even broken a sweat."

"I work out regularly." Gavin squeezed her hand. "I enjoy a good climb. Want me to carry you?" He raised a dark brow.

"The situation isn't that desperate yet. But there are steps inside the tower, too. I may take you up on it then." At the top of the hill, they admired the view of the Bay Bridge and Gavin suggested that maybe they'd climbed far enough.

"No way. You think I can't hack it, don't you?" She flexed her muscles under her new striped shirt. "I'd be a lousy date if we didn't even make it in to see all the murals. Did you hear the rumor that the tower was designed to look like a giant fire hose nozzle? Supposedly the lady who donated the land and the money to build the tower was a big fan of the local firehouse."

Gavin chuckled. "I can see a resemblance. I'm sure Sigmund Freud would have some other suggestions for things it looks like."

"You're not the first person to have made that observation, either. A giant phallic symbol rising over San Francisco. On that note, shall we go in?" She grinned and Gavin chuckled.

Inside the rotunda of the tower, he slid his arm around her waist as they looked at the murals painted during the depression: rural scenes of people picking crops, a San Francisco street scene complete with a pickpocket and a nasty car accident, a poor family panning for gold while a rich family looks on. "These were all painted during the depression, to provide work for artists, under the Works Progress Administration."

She enjoyed the warm sensation of his big arm around her, heating her skin through her thin blouse. "I know. Aren't they're stunning? I guess something good comes out of even the worst disasters."

"That's a very positive perspective. I fully approve." He squeezed her slightly as he turned to answer. Their faces hovered close for a second. Bree held her breath, sure he was going to lean in and kiss her...

But he peeled his arm gently from around her waist and moved away to peer at a detail in one of the paintings.

She rocked back on her boot heels and sucked in air. If he didn't make a move soon, she was going to go out of her mind.

After they had a delicious dinner and walked the short distance back to Russian Hill, Bree eased herself into the passenger seat of Gavin's sports car with a growing sense of anticipation and terror.

What if he *didn't* try anything? She might just die.

Gavin's gray gaze drifted from her hot cheeks

to her rather dramatic cleavage and back again, with enjoyment that made excitement sizzle in her belly.

She could hardly believe how intimate and easy their conversation had become over the last few dates. Weren't men supposed to be difficult and mysterious and hard to understand? Gavin was easier to talk to than her girlfriends.

His apartment was in a tall white building on Stockton Street, and they parked in the lot underneath.

"This is very convenient." Bree pressed the elevator button that Gavin said would take them from the garage up to his apartment. "I hardly feel like we're in San Francisco. Shouldn't you have to throw on the parking brake and hike up a hill to get home?"

Gavin grinned ruefully. "Until I met you, I'd been missing out on a lot of the city's charm. I moved in here so I'd be close to work. I've been in this apartment since I first came from L.A. five years ago."

Gavin stepped into the small elevator after her,

his nearness intimate in the cramped space. He'd rolled up his sleeves to reveal muscled forearms. His skin was tanned, dusted with dark hair. She wondered what those arms would feel like wrapped tight around her waist—right now.

Heat unfurled in her belly at the thought.

She glanced shyly at him as the door opened.

"We're here. It's the third door on the right. Not nearly as stylish as your studio, I'm afraid."

Bree walked down a hallway lined with identical blue doors. She watched Gavin's strong fingers turn the key in the lock, and a shimmer of exhilaration slid through her as he opened the door into his apartment.

Gavin held the door for Bree to walk in ahead of him and she could swear she felt his eyes on her backside as she stepped over the threshold. His interest in her put a swing in her hips that she'd never felt before.

The front door led into a living room dominated by a black leather sofa. A glass coffee table held three neat advertising magazines and a TV remote.

"Would you like a drink?" Gavin headed for the small kitchen. "I have white wine, vodka and rum."

"I think I'd better go for wine. I'm not used to the hard stuff." Just being around Gavin made her light-headed. She followed him into a neat galley kitchen with gleaming appliances. "Your apartment is very tidy."

"We can thank the maid for that. I'm not home all that much. I've been working flat out on the Prentice account lately. They're running a new campaign starting next month."

"I can't imagine working such long hours. You must be exhausted."

Gavin poured wine into two glasses and handed her one. "Not really. You get used to it. I enjoy the work—it's energizing for me."

She took the glass and smiled. "You're lucky to have found work you like so much."

"Trust me, I know it. We're both lucky that way. Here's to your promising career as one of

the West Coast's hottest young photographers."
He raised his glass and Bree clinked hers against
it.

"I'm not sure I'm really young enough for that
title."

"Of course you are. Don't be ridiculous."
Then a mock frown darkened his brow. "Unless
you're seventy and have a really good plastic
surgeon."

Bree laughed. "This is California. You should
probably check my driver's license."

"Nah. I'll take my chances and drink to
California's most beautiful photographer instead." He sipped his wine and peered at her
with those seductive gray eyes.

"Now you're just exaggerating."

"Not at all." His eyes swept over her, scorch-
ing her skin all the way from her exposed neck
to where her new expensive jeans encased her
thighs. "You're certainly the most gorgeous
woman in San Francisco, and I can say that
with some authority since I meet a lot of models

in my line of work. They'd all fade into the background with you around."

Bree bit her lip. What a flatterer. He did working in advertising—and she'd better not forget it. Still, he was very convincing.

She sipped her wine. The tart, cool liquid zinged over her tongue. Maybe he really did think she was pretty. She pushed her shoulders back the way Elle had shown her and tossed her curls behind her shoulders.

"Come sit on the sofa."

Gavin led her back into the living room. His blue striped shirt revealed his broad shoulders and, tucked into his faded jeans, emphasized his trim waist and a very cute butt. Desire sizzled in her belly as she imagined what he looked like underneath. All their hiking around the city had revealed him to be extremely fit.

She tore her gaze from his physique as he turned around and gestured for her to sit. She lowered herself carefully onto the leather couch and crossed her legs. Once again she felt Gavin's eyes on her cleavage. Heat swelled in her breasts and thickened her nipples, making them hum with sensation.

Usually she hated her large breasts. They were always in the way, making her feel large and ungainly. But in her new, perfectly fitting bra, they were transformed into a pleasant and desirable part of a body she was forming a new relationship with.

Since she'd met Gavin, she felt comfortable—sexy—in her own skin. For the first time in her life.

He put his glass down on the table. Feeling a sense of impending…something, Bree set hers next to it.

Her skin prickled as he drew closer. His scent, masculine and seductive, crept over her. She could see the shadow of stubble on his skin—he'd definitely have to shave twice a day to lose it. A tiny smile lifted the corners of his wide, sensual mouth.

Oh, boy.

Bree sucked in a breath as lips moved closer. *He's going to kiss me.*

Her heart beat hard against her ribs.

For an agonizing instant, their faces hovered so close she could feel the heat from his skin against her cheek. Panic rushed through her, laced with longing so deep it ached in her bones.

Then his mouth brushed softly against hers.

Four

Bree shuddered as sensation crashed through her. Gavin's big, strong hands pulled her close as he deepened the kiss. His fingers pressed into her back, revealing the urgency of his own need.

Their tongues met in a jolt of electricity and she enjoyed the rough rasp of his chin against hers. She writhed on the smooth leather, desire filling her body like a bottle that might overflow.

Her hands found their way to Gavin's shirt front, where she ran her fingertips over the cotton, feeling the muscle beneath.

A moan issued from his mouth and echoed through her. His thickly muscled arms pulled her close until her nipples brushed against his chest. Arousal thrummed low in her belly, pounding in a way she'd never felt before. Her hands were now on his back, roaming and testing the hard muscle, grasping at his shirt while he kissed her—hard and fast.

When they finally came up for air, Bree found herself blinking and breathless.

"Wow." The single, low syllable fell from Gavin's moistened lips.

Bree exhaled hard. "*Wow* is right." Her whole body stung and tingled with stray sensations all the way down to her toes.

She'd kissed men before, but it had never felt anything like this. Usually there was some groping and fumbling, and she'd even had rather disappointing sex on two occasions, but she'd never known anything like this crazy jumble of emotions and feelings that swept through her like madness.

She reached for her wine and took a bracing

gulp. Anticipation glowed between them in the quiet apartment. It wasn't total silence, though—the rapid beating of her heart warred with the ticking of a nearby clock.

Bree blew a lock of hair out of her face. "I guess that's what they call chemistry."

Gavin's mouth quirked into a smile. "No question. And I suspect if harnessed correctly it could solve all the world's energy problems."

"Less dangerous than nuclear fission, too."

"Or so we think." His storm-gray eyes swept over her. Her skin tingled as atoms snapped in half under his gaze. "Further experimentation is required."

Bree inhaled slowly, her breasts rising inside the caress of her bra. "If it's for the cause of science, we can hardly refuse." Her lips hummed with the desire to meet his again.

Gavin leaned in, his soft breath warming her skin for a second before his mouth slid over hers. Their tongues tangled and their hands grew bolder. Bree's fingertips slid beneath the waist of his pants and pulled at his shirt. She gasped when he brushed her nipple, and he cupped her breast, testing its weight in his palm.

Bree pulled his soft shirt loose in the back and reached under it, touching his skin. It was hotter than she expected, and the muscles of his back flexed under her fingertips.

His thumb slipped inside her blouse and strummed her nipple through her bra. She arched and moaned through their kiss in response.

Leaning into him, she let her fingernails rake over the hard muscle on either side of his spine. She'd never felt such a powerful male body. Heat simmered in her core as she felt the sheer strength of him, so different from the skinny boys she'd known in the past.

With a deft hand, he unbuttoned her blouse and pushed it aside until her breast was bared— or at least her bra. Her lips reluctantly gave up his mouth as Gavin pulled back.

Bree's eyes opened to see his gaze resting on her cleavage. The fine lace of the pretty bra gave the vista an erotic flavor. Thank goodness she wasn't wearing one of her old, white "over-the-shoulder-boulder-holders." She owed Elle big time for her fashion and beauty tips.

Gavin's chest rose as he inhaled and sighed. "This is the best view I've seen in a long time."

"And I bet you can see pretty far from this high floor."

"Rooftops and seagulls have nothing on the hills and valleys I see right now." His gaze scorched her skin. Then his fingers tugged at her blouse and pulled it off completely. Bree wriggled out of the sleeves, until she was naked from the waist up.

Well, a bra counted as naked, didn't it?

She certainly felt naked under his hungry gaze.

Gavin lowered his mouth to her breast and licked her nipple through the satiny fabric. Bree's belly quivered at the sensation. His hand roamed over her back, sliding under the bra strap, then releasing the clasp with practiced ease.

She sucked in a breath as he pulled the black

satin and lace from her, leaving her totally exposed.

"You are unbelievably hot." His eyes rested on her chest as he said it, which made her laugh. Her breasts weren't used to such frank and enthusiastic worship, and she couldn't help enjoying it.

"I don't think it's fair that only one of us gets to enjoy the view." She reached for his shirt buttons and pushed the shirt back to reveal ripped, tanned muscle. "Ah, much better."

A fine line of silky dark hair ran between his thick pecs, heading down below his leather belt. Bree's breath caught in her throat as she saw the thick bulge beneath the buckle.

On instinct, her hand slid down to touch him through the denim of his jeans. Hard and powerful, his raw arousal made her blink.

"I think we'd be more comfortable in the bedroom." Gavin's low voice sent a shiver of awareness through her.

"Okay." Her voice may have quavered a bit but he didn't seem to notice.

After a smoky head-to-toe glance that threatened to light her skin on fire, he took her hand and led her into his bedroom.

He switched on a soft light, which threw out just enough illumination to reveal dark blue sheets on a wide wooden bed with sleek modern lines. Blinds covered the floor-to-ceiling windows. Gavin shrugged off his shirt—which was barely on to begin with—and held out his hands. Bree walked into his inviting embrace.

Her skin hummed under his exploring fingers. Breathless and a little nervous, she reached for his belt buckle. She wasn't experienced but she knew she shouldn't sit back and wait for him to do everything. He was probably used to temptresses like that woman at the party, who could drive a man to heights of distraction with one flick of a manicured fingernail.

She was surprised when the thick leather belt came easily through the thin buckle. Her knuckles grazed his thick erection, which throbbed under her touch.

He really wants me. She still could hardly

believe it. How could everything have turned around so quickly?

One minute she was plain old Bree Kincannon, going about her usual dull but pleasant existence. Now she was standing in a strange man's apartment in her underwear, apparently on the brink of making love.

Love?

No. No one had said anything about love. Still, she couldn't deny that she felt a special connection with Gavin. And he obviously felt it, too. Isn't this what falling in love must be like?

"Oh!" She let out a little exclamation of surprise as he unzipped her jeans. He slid them down her thighs, caressing her skin with his mouth as he went, leaving her in only her lace-edged panties.

"You're breathtaking," he murmured.

Bree tried to hold up her end by undoing his jeans. Her eager fingers fumbled with the button and Gavin helped her slide them over his tight backside and down his thick, powerful thighs.

Oh, my. She'd never seen thighs like that. At

least not outside an underwear commercial. Heart in her throat, she tugged at his dark gray boxers and couldn't help gasping as his arousal sprang free.

Gavin guided her gently onto the cool sheets and tugged her panties down over her thighs.

Now she really was naked. Excitement and fear prickled in her veins.

He climbed over her, his big muscled body making hers seem almost insubstantial, and lowered himself carefully onto the bed beside her.

A gentle kiss on the lips soothed her rattled nerves. Gavin's broad fingers roamed over her belly, leaving tingles of sensation in their wake. She tensed up slightly as he strayed between her thighs, but she parted her legs and let them in.

His fingertip probed into her warmth and she sucked in a breath as it found a sensitive spot. Her hips twitched slightly as he moved his fingers, stimulating secret places no one else had cared to explore.

Eyes closed, an expression of pleasure lighting

his chiseled features, Gavin looked more heart-breakingly handsome than ever. Bree's heart squeezed. Could he be the one?

She'd more or less given up hoping that Prince Charming would come sweep her off her feet. Every little girl has that dream, but a grown woman of twenty-nine has learned that most frogs don't improve all that much upon kissing.

Ooh. She wriggled as Gavin's fingers sent a shockwave zinging through her. A tiny moan escaped her lips. Gavin's eyes opened a crack, and a wicked smile played at the edges of his sensual mouth.

Hot and slick under his touch, she felt more aroused than ever in her life. Gavin eased closer, until their bodies pressed together all the way from his broad shoulders to his sturdy thighs. Then he raised himself up onto a powerful arm, rolled on a condom with expert ease, and climbed over her.

She couldn't help an involuntary shudder as he entered her. All her nerve endings were alive and buzzing. Eyes closed, she gave herself over to the sensation. Her fingers dug into the hard muscle of his back as he slid inside her, slow and gentle, opening her like a secret chamber left unexplored for far too long.

Once inside her, Gavin released a throaty moan—a sound of relief mingled with pleasure. He started to move, and Bree's hips automatically joined in the dance, just as her body had flowed with his so readily on the dance floor at the charity gala. Maybe they were meant to be together....

She let the delicious thought flow through her as she followed him into a new realm of pleasure. Gavin's hands roamed over her body, squeezing and enjoying every inch of her, as they moved together. She explored the muscled ridges of his back and the firm curve of his backside.

Desire fluttered in her chest—and in all kinds of places she didn't know existed—as Gavin deftly shifted them into different positions. Heat pulsed through her and her thoughts jumbled and scattered as primal sensation shoved thought aside. Her body cleaved to his, writhing and twisting, steamy and slick.

She arched under him, taking him deeper, her breath coming in unsteady gasps, until suddenly everything exploded.

Or imploded.

Her body convulsed and twitched as tidal waves of wringing pleasure crashed through her bloodstream.

Then a low groan filled the air and she felt Gavin's arms wrapped around her like a vice. He throbbed inside her, sending further sparks of nuclear fission to her fingers and toes.

"Wow." His voice, thick and rough, echoed her exclamation after their kiss.

"Uh-huh," she murmured back, half amazed that she could still use language. Her brain seemed to have switched off for a few moments there. She opened her eyelids a tiny bit and her gaze locked onto Gavin's. His gray eyes dark with passion, he gazed at her, wrapped up in her completely.

Bree's chest tightened, filled with too much emotion. Gavin Spencer was too much for her. Way too much. Sweet, kind, caring, thoughtful—and ridiculously handsome. Things like this didn't happen to her. She was boring old Bree, the one you could always count on in a pinch because you knew she'd be free.

Or was she?

Maybe, after Elle's clever alterations, and with the help of Gavin's experienced touch, she'd truly morphed and changed into someone new. Someone exciting and desirable, whose life would now unfurl and brighten like a flower after the rain.

"I've never met anyone quite like you, Bree." Gavin rested his head on the pillow, peering at her through sleepy, half-closed eyes.

"Me? There's nothing special about me." She kicked herself for giving in to the familiar urge to run herself down.

A frown furrowed Gavin's brow. "Everything about you is special." He stroked her chin with his thumb. "You're warm and kind and caring. You're clever and creative and artistic."

Bree swallowed. She'd heard those before. They were the kind of compliments her starchy aunts offered, usually after critiquing her posture and lamenting her lack of marital prospects.

"And you're the best looking woman in San Francisco."

"Only in San Francisco?" She couldn't help teasing. His smoky gaze roamed over her naked body making her feel like the most beautiful woman on earth.

"Definitely in the whole Bay area. And the State of California. And the entire West Coast."

Bree mock pouted. "And there I was hoping for the Midwest, as well."

"I haven't spent much time there so I'm not an authority." His narrowed gaze twinkled with mischief.

"Never mind then." She tossed her curls. Gavin took one in his fingers and tried it on like a ring. "That's rather suggestive," she murmured.

"Perhaps that's my intention." He cocked his head slightly.

She bit her lip to stop a naughty smile sneaking across her mouth. "Shouldn't we get some sleep? Tomorrow's a workday."

"Actually, I'm on vacation. Had to use it or lose it."

"Lucky you."

"But if you have a busy day, I quite understand." He twirled her curl softly around his finger.

"Actually, I don't." She didn't have any plans at all, in fact.

"Then I have an idea." His brow furrowed again. "A big idea. A crazy, mad, wonderful idea."

Curiosity prickled through Bree. "What?"

He shifted until he was sitting up. "I'll be right back."

With a navy towel around his waist, Gavin strode to the study.

Crazy.

Definitely crazy, but the idea had seized him.

Maybe because everything about Bree felt so right. Their lovemaking was sensational. Bree was every bit as passionate and erotic as he'd imagined, and that unbelievable body of hers.... He frowned at the erection already getting started again.

Mad.

No question he was mad. Everyone would tell him that. Heck, Bree would probably tell him that. They'd only known each other for two and a half weeks. But sometimes the universe was on your side and everything came together, like the time he won the big Stayco account.

No. This was nothing like the time he won the Stayco account. That was a business relationship. This would be a lifetime commitment.

His chest tightened. A lifetime with Bree. Right now that seemed very appealing.

In the study, the display on the digital clock gave off just enough illumination for him to see the drawer handles.

Yes, the one million dollars offered by her father was an enticement. But it wasn't the only one, not by any means. It was more like a pearl necklace around the neck of a beautiful woman: it enhanced her appeal, rather than overshadowed it.

Wonderful.

That's how things could be if everything went according to plan. He and Bree could buy a nice house somewhere—maybe even Russian Hill, he'd always liked that area.

He could finally start his own company and settle into an exciting yet comfortable existence as a man in charge of his own destiny.

Excitement swelled inside him. He pulled open the top drawer and reached into its dark interior. Past the paper clips and stapler, his fingertips settled on a smooth leather box. He picked it up. The gold embossed around the edges glowed in the green light from the clock. He'd had no idea what to do with this ring when he was given it, but suddenly it seemed like just another perfectly fitting piece in the puzzle of his life.

He flipped open the lid to reveal a lovely Art Deco ring, three flawless diamonds—a large one flanked by two smaller ones—in a pretty setting. Most people probably would have sold it, but he couldn't do that. It had belonged to his grandmother, one of the most amazing people he'd ever met. She'd encouraged his creative ambitions, taking him to drama class and music lessons, paying for summer arts camp when his parents had disapproved.

She'd left him the ring in her will. At the time he'd wondered why, but now he knew. She wanted him to give it to the woman he loved.

Gavin drew in a ragged breath and plucked the ring from its satin bed. Would Bree be offended by the offer of a used ring? She was an heiress, after all, able to buy whatever she wanted without a thought.

The ring glittered as he examined it. Bree wasn't flashy or pretentious, he thought. Deep down, he suspected the sentimental value of a ring might be more important than its market price.

He had no idea if it would fit, but that would

be easy enough to fix. He left the box on the desk and tucked the ring into his palm.

Bree lay on the bed, curls sprawled on the pillow, the sheet draped over her delicious body. She smiled as he stood in the doorway. Adrenaline surged through Gavin's body—how would she react? Might she reject him out of hand? Then his plans would lie in ruins and he'd have to tell her father he'd failed to hold up his part of the bargain.

Her dark lashes flickered as she looked at him, expectant, probably wondering why he stood over her, hesitating, one hand behind his back. The ring prickled against his skin, hard facets of diamond goading him to ask her his burning question.

He walked to the bed and sat down on the covers next to her. The heat from her skin warmed him and eased the tension in his limbs. "Bree, I know we haven't known each other long." His voice sounded oddly gruff. Her eyes widened. "But sometimes life offers you a rare opportunity, something you weren't expecting and couldn't even have hoped for." He swallowed. "Bree, will you marry me?"

Five

Bree blinked. Obviously she was asleep and dreaming.

But it felt so real.

Gavin sat next to her on the bed, muscles honed by the soft lamplight, a towel wrapped around his waist like a toga. In his fingers, something sparkled. A ring. Just like in fairy tales when the handsome prince gets down on one knee and…

"I know it's sudden." His voice interrupted her thoughts. "I'm sure you're surprised. I am, too. I had no idea I could develop such strong feelings for a woman so quickly."

Chest tightening, Bree pushed herself up onto one elbow. "I'm not dreaming, am I?"

Gavin's handsome features creased into a smile. "No, you're not. I'm as real as you are." He caressed her thigh through the sheet. Her skin hummed under his touch.

"And I'd like you to be my wife."

She swallowed. Gavin Spencer wanted to marry her? This couldn't be real. For a start, they'd known each other less than three weeks. Plus, he was gorgeous, a drop-dead knockout who must have women trailing after him wherever he went. Why would he want to be stuck with one woman for the rest of his life—least of all her?

"It's too sudden, isn't it?" He tilted his head.

"No. I mean, I don't know." She had no idea how to respond. Did she want to marry him? All the nerves and muscles in her body—especially those newly awakened by the evening's activities—sang *yes!* in a harmonized chorus.

But the old Bree muttered something quite different. *Beware. Something's off here. It's too soon. He's too good to be true.*

Bree drew in a long breath, which didn't help steady her racing nerves. "I don't know what to say." Her voice came out high and squeaky.

"'Yes' would work." Gavin's gray eyes sparkled, much like the glittering ring in his palm. Odd that it lay flat in his hand. Didn't men in the movies usually hold it between their fingers?

But this wasn't a movie. It was her life. Which had suddenly taken such a strange turn that she hardly knew who she was anymore, let alone how she should react.

"But we only just met. You don't know me." What if he married her, then realized she was just boring old Bree, not the fantasy woman he'd built up in his mind? "You probably think I'm a lot more exciting and interesting than I really am."

Gavin cocked his head. "You should have more faith in yourself." He eased closer on the bed and rested his free hand at her waist. "We've spent hours talking and you're undoubtedly the most thoughtful, intelligent and interesting person I've ever met."

"Am I really?" The question flew out before she could stop it. How embarrassing to go fishing for a compliment like that.

"No question about it. And that's not all. I'm entranced by your beauty, too."

"Oh, come on." She blushed. "I'm hardly a head turner."

"That's where you are so wrong. Heads turn wherever you go."

Bree bit her lip. Elle's makeover had apparently had its intended effect. She'd never attracted so much attention in her life as she had in the past couple of weeks. Even the time she'd accidentally worn two unmatched shoes to school on Awards Day.

"I'd be a good husband."

"I'm sure you would."

But doubts still niggled. Why was he trying so hard to sell himself? Couldn't they date for a while and test each other out more?

"I'd cherish and honor and ravish you." A mischievous gleam lit his eyes. A flash of desire echoed in Bree's belly. "Why don't you just try it on?" He shrugged, as if it was something casual. Try on an engagement ring and see how the whole engagement experience feels.

Bree shrugged, trying to conceal the odd mass of feelings roiling in her stomach.

"Why not?" Her squeaky voice betrayed her apprehension.

Gavin held the ring for her. She raised her hand. She rarely wore jewelry at all, and never on that finger. Everyone knew it was bad luck to put anything but an engagement ring on it. She'd never really expected to put a ring on that finger, resigned as she was to her quiet life with her cats.

Now a new realm of possibilities glittered, facets shimmering in the dim light. She poked out her naked finger, clutching the sheets about her with her other hand. A shiver of fear and excitement slashed through her as the cool metal touched her skin. Would it be too small? She wasn't a petite little thing, though her hands were probably the most delicate part of her. Would it stick firm over a knuckle and refuse to budge?

That would be a sign.

But it slid on, smoothly, all the way to the right spot.

"A perfect fit." Gavin's triumphant gaze fixed on hers.

"It is. How did you manage that?"

"Pure luck. And I think it's a message from the universe that it fits so well." He stroked her hand where the ring glittered on her finger. "I don't know how you'll feel about this, but it's a special ring. It belonged to my grandmother, who was married to the love of her life for fifty-seven years."

The three stones sat in a pretty setting. Looking at it now, she could see it was probably designed in the twenties. "It's lovely."

The ring buzzed a little against her skin. She wasn't sure how she felt about wearing someone else's wedding ring. It seemed to underscore the sensation that she'd accidentally stepped into someone else's life.

"My grandmother was very special to me. She gave me the ring in her will so I could give it to my wife one day. I can't believe how well it fits you. Like it was made for you."

Bree gulped. Now that the ring was on her finger, did that mean she'd said yes? "It's beautiful. Are you sure you want to part with it?"

Gavin held her hand. "I don't want to part with it. I want it on the finger of the woman I love."

Bree's stomach clenched. The word *love* hung in the air like a flash of smoke from a magic trick.

That's what had been missing, why the whole proposal had felt rather odd, forced—because he hadn't told her he loved her.

Until now.

"I love you, Bree." He caressed her hand with his thumb. "It's a new love, untried and untested, I'll admit. But I've never felt like this about anyone before. Something in my gut, in my heart, tells me that you're the woman for me."

The conviction in his voice wrapped around her like a cloak. Did she love him? She had no idea what love was even supposed to feel like. Arousal and desire sizzled through her like steam, no denying that. And Gavin was sweet and charming and intelligent and fun. And completely hot.

All the things she would have looked for in her dream husband. If she was looking for a husband. Which she certainly should be, according to pretty much everyone she knew. She was just so used to being suspicious, to doubting the motives of any man who came near her because he might be more interested in the Kincannon coffers than in her.

"There's something special between us, isn't there?" His voice interrupted her thoughts.

"Yes, there is." Bree frowned. The connection between them crackled right now, as she sat on the bed, her hands in his. She'd never felt so comfortable with a man, so safe. She'd certainly never felt so desirable and intriguing. "I do feel it."

She looked down at the three diamonds twinkling on her finger.

"Will you marry me?" Gavin's simple question, asked with hope in his wide gray gaze, blew away any last traces of resistance.

"Yes. I will." Exhilaration—and terror—flashed through her as she said the words. But she also felt a fierce conviction that this was right. Strange—and sudden—as it was, their pairing was meant to be.

Gavin wrapped his arms around her and held her tight. The warmth from his body mingled with hers and possibly for the first time in her life—at least since her mother died—she felt totally protected and cared for.

And loved.

As they pulled onto the Golden Gate Bridge in Gavin's car, Bree snuck a glance backward at the city. When she returned, she'd be a married woman. Mrs. Gavin Spencer. They were getting married right over the bridge in Sausalito.

Gavin had wanted to get married as soon as

possible. No guests, just the two of them—and Bree's cats. Gavin had sweetly insisted that they come, too, since they were members of the family. One of his former clients owned a boutique hotel with a terrace overlooking the city that hosted small weddings quite often. He'd promised to provide the wedding officiant, a photographer and two witnesses.

The whole thing had been arranged so fast. The only holdup was the prenup—Gavin had insisted on one, maybe to prove that he wasn't a gold digger. She found the whole thing embarrassing. Didn't it imply that they might one day get divorced? She didn't want to think about that. Still, he'd managed to get one drawn up and signed in less than a day, and now here they were, barely forty-eight hours after his proposal.

Gavin turned to look at her. "Nervous?"

"A little." It was all happening so quickly. And a wedding without any friends and family seemed odd.

Still, despite some reservations, Bree had

to admit it made sense. She didn't want the kind of big society wedding her father would have insisted on, which would take a full year to plan and involve more fuss than a royal inauguration. Better to do it this way, quickly and privately. Oddly, her father hadn't protested their impromptu plans the way she'd expected. He'd seemed quite unsurprised by her news and happy for both of them. Which wasn't so odd, really, since he'd undoubtedly introduced her to Gavin in the hope that she'd finally find a mate. Finally she'd managed to accomplish something her father approved of! Or at least she would have soon.

Very soon.

"Sausalito's a fun place to escape to. Even though it's just across the bridge, you feel like you're a million miles away." His warm grin tickled something inside her. Gavin looked even more breathtaking than usual today. A casual black shirt rolled up over his powerful forearms, faded jeans, his thick, dark hair slightly tousled. She could hardly believe she was sitting next to him, let alone driving to Sausalito to marry him.

The diamond ring still glittered on her finger. She hadn't taken it off since he'd put it on to test the size.

"We can live in my condo until we find a place. But I think we should get a house, so there will be plenty of room for you to have a big studio. What do you think?"

"I don't know what to think." She smiled. "I've never lived anywhere but the house I'm in now. I'm open to anything. I can always rent a separate studio for my business."

"No way. We'll find a house with a great studio for you. And a view of the bay is a must, since you're used to enjoying one."

How rich was he? He talked as if he had all the funds in the world at his disposal. Or did he expect her to pay for their new house? Odd how they were about to walk down the aisle but they hadn't discussed even the most basic practical matters.

Except the prenup. And those often weren't

worth the paper they were written on anyway. If he hadn't insisted, she wouldn't even have thought of it. If she couldn't trust her husband, who could she trust? She wouldn't let money rule her life.

They drove through the low hills of the Gateway National Recreation area, then climbed up into the steep and picturesque streets of Sausalito. He pulled up in the circular driveway of a small Mediterranean style building with blooms bursting from pots and beds in every direction.

"The wedding's booked for six o'clock tonight, so we'll have plenty of time to get ready."

"Tonight?" Panic flashed over Bree. For some reason she assumed they'd have at least a day to…to what? If they were getting married, might as well get on with it.

Still, she'd barely had a chance to get used to having a "fiancé" yet, and they were going to run down the aisle *tonight*. Kind of funny how he'd just gone ahead and made all the plans—and she'd let him.

Gavin climbed out of the car, then came around to open her door. She stepped out onto the gravel on shaky legs. He slid a palm across the base of her spine, which sent waves of heat—as well as anxiety—shivering through her. "Tonight will be our wedding night." His smoky gray gaze smoldered with possibilities.

Bree blinked and blew out a shaky breath. "So it will."

He squeezed her hand. "I can't wait to be your husband, Bree."

"I can't wait to be your wife." She squeezed back, and happiness swelled in her chest, pushing away the anxiety. He was so open and affectionate, on top of all the other things she adored about him. Did anyone have a right to be this lucky?

Then she froze. "But what am I going to wear?"

"Anything you like. We have all afternoon to shop."

* * *

Though Bree was nervous about her ability to pick a flattering dress without Elle, she found one quite easily at a stylish shop down near the docks. The silvery-white, tea-length gown in shimmering satin draped elegantly over her curves. Sky-blue heels proved an oddly perfect match. At a local jeweler, they chose engraved wedding bands for the ceremony. Back at the hotel, she was visited by a bubbly hairdresser who piled her curls into a chignon fastened with pearl-tipped pins. Bree put on the sparkly pearl and diamond earrings they'd picked together. Gavin insisted on paying for everything, and her transformation into a blushing bride gave him obvious delight.

"You're breathtaking." He came up behind her as she put the finishing touches on her lipstick. His face appearing next to hers in the mirror made her smile.

"You're pretty smashing yourself." She glanced at his crisp, black satin bowtie. The elegant tuxedo only enhanced his matinee-idol good looks.

"We do make a nice looking couple." He slid his arms around her satin clad waist.

"And we do fit well together." She didn't look at all big or ungainly next to him—at over six feet, he made her feel perfectly proportioned. She wriggled under his tempting, warm touch. "In fact, I rather wish we didn't have to leave the room."

"It'll be worth it." He pressed a soft kiss to her cheek. Her skin, already hot and made up with blush, flushed deeper under his lips. "And we'll have all night to celebrate." Gavin's throaty whisper echoed through her, a promise of sensations she was quickly becoming addicted to. "Are you ready?"

"As ready as I'll ever be."

Panic and excitement tingled to Bree's toes and fingers as they stepped out onto the hotel's terrace. Glorious sunshine lit up the simple gazebo where the officiant waited for them.

Gavin tightened his reassuring grip on her hand, and shot her an encouraging glance. Petunias spilled from carved pots and planters, and ribbons festooned the table holding the official paperwork.

The hotel's manager walked up to them, followed by a pretty blonde holding a boutonniere for Gavin. "Welcome, and congratulations on your special day." The speech sounded a little canned, Bree thought, then cursed herself for the petty thought. They were just being polite, and trying to make them feel at home.

She glanced out at the impressive view over the bay, where sailboats scudded over the dark water. It was a lovely spot to get married. Perfect, even. Besides, the whole point was to join herself to this wonderful man and begin an exciting new chapter in her life.

Still, her breathing came a little shallow as they walked toward the gazebo where the officiant stood waiting.

Could something that came together this quickly and easily really be permanent? Despite

Gavin's strong and soothing hand in hers, Bree found herself pestered by doubts.

Maybe Gavin thought he was marrying the ringleted temptress Elle had turned her into, rather than the real her. What would happen when he discovered he'd married a dull mouse rather than the exciting woman of his dreams?

"I love you, Bree." His whispered words banished her worries like a strong breeze.

"I love you, too, Gavin." She rasped the words back with conviction. How had he known to turn and reassure her at just the right moment?

Because he was perfect—for her.

A few pleasantries were exchanged, and before she had a chance to gather her wits, the ceremony was underway.

"Do you, Bree Kincannon, take this man to be your lawfully wedded husband, to have and to hold, to cherish and love, as long as you both shall live?"

"I do." She spoke the words clear and loud, determined not to let any lingering doubts become evident to the witnesses, even if they

were strangers. Gavin said his vows with a reassuring, deep voice and an expression of honest
enthusiasm that almost made her laugh aloud.

"You may now kiss the bride."

In front of the assembled strangers, Gavin
eased his arms around her waist, pulled her
close, and kissed her—gentle, yet firm. Heat
shimmered through her from head to toe.

"We're married," he whispered. "I've never
felt so excited and happy in my whole life."

"Me, either." Bree spoke the truth. A whirlwind wedding to the most gorgeous man she'd
ever met was unquestionably the high point of
her quiet life so far. "It's all happened so quickly,
I can't quite believe it."

"When something's right, it's like all the forces
in the universe converge to make everything
come together. That force has been in motion
since the moment I met you."

"Even though I was wearing that horrid gray
dress?"

Gavin laughed. "An ordinary dress can't hide
the light that shines from inside you, Bree. I

could tell right away that you were special. And then when we danced…" He let out a low whistle that tickled a laugh from down deep in her belly. "We're definitely going out dancing later." Then he hesitated. "Or maybe tomorrow. It's our wedding night and I have some very detailed plans for it." A slightly raised brow made desire quiver in Bree. The promise of sensual pleasure thickened her nipples under her silky dress.

She almost slid her hand inside his jacket to enjoy the hot hard muscle she knew lay under his elegant tux.

Then she remembered they still stood in the middle of the hotel terrace, under the professional gaze of the "witnesses."

She glanced around and took a step back. "Perhaps we should go somewhere more private?"

Back in their comfortable suite, which also featured breathtaking views of the bay, Gavin had the whole evening arranged down to the finest detail. Even the cats were settled near the sofa with gourmet meals and plush cushions. A knock on the door confirmed that everything was happening according to plan.

"That must be dinner." He kissed Bree's sweet lips one more time before heading for the door to their suite. He'd secretly placed an order for the hotel's finest meal, for them to enjoy in the privacy of their suite.

Only the best for Bree. Not because she was an heiress and accustomed to it anyway, but because he truly did want to cherish her, and to see that pretty face light with its familiar glowing smile.

"I'd just assumed we'd go out." Bree glanced at the door.

"On our wedding night? I prefer privacy." He shot her a teasing glance.

The waiter wheeled in a cart laden with pretty Mediterranean pottery, then congratulated them and left. Bree lifted the lid of the first dish to reveal a rush of steam and the tempting scent of delicate hors d'oeuvres, two of each, an array of tiny pastries and bite-sized morsels.

He fed them to Bree, and she returned the favor, both of them laughing. When had he ever done anything this simple—this silly—with a woman, and had such a great time?

Never. That's when.

Bree's easy, drama-free approach to life was so refreshing. Even if one million big ones weren't currently winging their way into his bank account, he'd be very pleased with his choice of a life partner.

The soup was creamy vichyssoise sprinkled with fresh chives. Tender steak tips, baby vegetables and new potatoes in a rich gravy made a satisfying main course, and he was sure he couldn't eat another thing until they uncovered the desserts—tiny éclairs and profiteroles, delicate tarts and hand-decorated cakes. He licked cream off Bree's lips and toasted their marriage with a glass of Moet.

"I think we should retire to the bedroom." He picked up the champagne and their two glasses. "We'll be more comfortable there."

He waited while she stood, looking radiant,

glowing like a movie star in her wedding finery. So different from the quiet, almost apologetic woman he'd met that first night at the gala. She'd blossomed magnificently since he met her. Eyes darted toward her wherever they went, taking in her statuesque beauty, and she looked quite comfortable and assured under the gaze of all those envious males.

The bed was turned down, fresh white sheets gleaming in the soft light. Bree settled herself gingerly on the edge and accepted the offered glass of champagne.

Gavin sat down next to her and pulled a pearl-tipped pin from her chignon. "Rapunzel, Rapunzel, let down your hair."

She giggled. "Wouldn't it be a shame to undo all the hairdresser's hard work?"

"But I can't run my hands through your tresses when they're all piled up on your head." He pulled out another pin, this one with a spray of baby pearls around a tiny diamond. A single coiled ringlet tumbled free.

Bree tugged gently at one end of his bow tie.

It slid apart and she pulled the black silk loose from his collar. "Two can play at that game." Her green eyes glittered, pupils wide and dark.

The flame of desire burning deep inside Gavin all day roared through his muscles. But he kept his cool and slowly pulled another pin from Bree's shiny updo. A thick lock of luscious dark hair fell to her shoulder.

Bree reached for the button on his collar and pulled it loose. She undid the next one and ran a cool finger along his chest between his pecs.

Arousal snapped inside him. He lifted the fallen lock of hair and found the delicate shoulder strap of her dress. Pushing it aside, he kissed her shoulder and neck, inhaling the rich scent of her and burying his face in her hair. "Bree, you drive me crazy."

"Crazy enough to make you marry me, apparently."

"I'm the luckiest man alive." He found the zipper on the side of her dress and tugged it down gently. "To have the woman of my dreams right here in my arms."

Or in his hands. He let them roam, shameless and hungry for the touch of her after a day of restraint. His palms cupped her full, heavy breasts, sending desire pounding through him like a drumbeat. He slid his hands to her hips, to enjoy the lush curves draped in seductive satin. Breathing ragged, he pressed a hot kiss to her mouth.

Bree pushed herself against him, breasts crushing against his chest, her hands tangling under his jacket. "Your clothes are in the way," she gasped, when they broke for air.

She shoved his jacket off onto the floor and yanked at the last buttons on his shirt, then pushed it back over his shoulders.

Half blind with desire, Gavin helped Bree out of her shimmering dress until she lay sprawled on the bed, a vision of lush skin and delicate white lace underwear. Her hair tumbled about her face in gorgeous disarray.

Her tugged her bra straps down one at a time, then unhooked the bra to reveal her tight, pink nipples. He eased her panties down inch by inch, enjoying the soft curves of her hips and thighs. Her skin tasted honey sweet, like nectar against his tongue.

Bree wriggled under his teasing tongue until she reached up and grabbed him around the waist. They met, skin to skin, in a delicious collision. Hard and ready, he kissed her as she welcomed him into her slick warmth.

She arched her back and made a tiny sound as he sank into her, a murmur of pure pleasure that filled him with joy. "I love you, Bree," he rasped, meaning every word.

"I love you, too." Their bodies tangled along with their words, hot and heartfelt, in a dance that celebrated their whirlwind affair and wedding.

No matter how it started, this romance would take them both to the stars.

Six

Breakfast in bed followed by slow, lazy love-making was a great way to start the day. Bree brushed croissant crumbs from the sheets, then trailed her fingers over Gavin's chest. Oddly enough, being married to him felt totally natural. Maybe all the hot, sticky sex had somehow glued them together.

"Why are you laughing?" His chest rumbled under her fingers.

"Private joke."

"Shouldn't those be shared between husband and wife?" He cocked a brow at her.

"I don't know. I've never been married before."
She grinned.

"Me, either. I think that means we get to make
up all the rules as we go along. Rule one, we
should take a shower together."

Bree smiled. "That shower is big enough
for two." Gavin whisked her off the bed and
carried her in his arms into the shimmering
white marble bathroom. He opened the glass
door of the shower and adjusted the controls,
all while holding her crooked between his arm
and knee.

"You're making me feel downright dainty."

"You're downright delicious." He nipped at
her neck with his teeth and laid a trail of kisses
to her mouth. Warm water splashed from the
gold faucets and spattered them both with tiny
droplets. Bree licked some off his chest. His
skin tasted salty and savory, and soon she was
on her feet, kissing him hard, with water raining
down over both of them.

They lathered each other with silky jasmine
scented soap and rinsed by hand, until each

individual body part was squeaky clean. With Gavin's hands on her, and his eyes greedily reveling in the way the water cascaded between her breasts, she felt like a goddess.

Desire shimmered in every cell of her body, keeping her in a constant state of peak arousal. Gavin was as hard as a Renaissance statue, built with curves and angles every bit as artistic. Water poured over his olive skin and trickled along the line of dark hair that enhanced the sculpted muscles of his chest.

His hands roamed over her, soapy and slick, treasuring her like a precious object. She still couldn't believe her luck. Apparently he couldn't get enough of her. And the feeling was entirely mutual. She'd never imagined wanting to spend a whole morning kissing and making love—after a full night of the same. The sheer pleasure that tingled through her was an addictive drug that made her crave Gavin's skin on hers.

They teased and touched and licked each other until the intensity of the arousal became overwhelming. Groaning with sheer relief, Gavin entered her and they both reached their climax almost immediately, under the soft rain of water.

"You're perfect, Bree. Perfect," he moaned, shuddering in her arms as they leaned heavily against the tiled wall. It was all Bree could do to stay upright. Her muscles had turned to water and her brain was too light with joy to form thoughts.

"You're…amazing." She couldn't even come up with a description for the man who'd turned her life inside out and made her…happy. Happier than she'd ever imagined possible. Dreams really did come true, just when you least expected it.

They spent that day and the next enjoying the sights of Sausalito. A boat ride on the bay, an exquisite French meal and a night of dancing in a steamy local club.

Everywhere they went people seemed to smile at them as if they glowed with some special newlywed happiness. Which they probably did.

It's all too good to be true. He's too good to be true.

Whenever the sneaky doubts crept around the edges of her brain, Bree banished them with a swat. It was just the old insecurities creeping back, the years of being an ugly duckling, attractive to men only for her money.

But Gavin didn't need her money. He seemed to have no interest in it at all. He was successful in his own right. She could be as poor as a church mouse and it didn't make any difference to him.

She laughed aloud. Gavin, marching up one of the punishingly steep hills next to her, turned and squeezed her hand. "This time I won't even ask why you're laughing."

"Why not?"

"Because I know." A broad smile lit his handsome face. "I feel exactly the same way."

Back in San Francisco, Bree went to her apartment to pack a few necessities into her car and bring them to Gavin's. His apartment was roomy enough for all of them—her cat Faith wound herself around Gavin's legs, purring, then settled happily into a sunny spot by the living room window. Even the more reserved Ali seemed calm and quickly claimed a big soft armchair as her new home.

Now they officially lived together.

"Do you realize I never had the opportunity to live in sin?" She poked him gently with her finger as they lay in his bed, after their first night in their temporary home.

"I'm so sorry to have deprived you. I'm sure we can come up with some other sins to indulge in."

"Isn't it odd how nonchalant my dad was about the whole thing? He didn't seem at all surprised when I told him we were getting married. He must really like you. He hasn't introduced me to a man in a long time."

"He knows a good son-in-law when he sees one." Gavin's gray eyes twinkled.

"It's particularly amazing that he didn't mind us running off to Sausalito to get married without any big fanfare. He's usually such a snob about how things are done."

"Maybe he's just glad to see you happily settled." Gavin twirled a lock of her hair.

"I suppose so. Maybe it's a weight off his mind that I won't be a bitter spinster living in the garret of his house for the rest of his life." She grinned. "I much prefer being a happily married woman."

"Well, your happily married husband needs to get to work." Gavin eased away from her. Already her skin buzzed with protest, missing the contact with his.

"I'm not sure I can stand to be away from you all day." She pouted and pulled the sheets over her.

"We could meet for lunch." Gavin climbed out of bed and strode across the room, all toned muscle and easy grace. "That might be enough to prevent withdrawal from setting in."

"No. I'll be stoic." Bree tossed her head against the pillow dramatically. "I know your work is important to you and I don't want to be a distraction. Which of your big accounts are you working on today?"

An odd expression flickered across Gavin's face as he reached for his shirt. "Hmm. Not sure. All thoughts of Maddox Communications have fled my mind."

"You'd better hunt them down before Brock Maddox realizes. I'm glad I've met all the people you work with. Now, when you tell me about your day, I'll know exactly who you mean."

"Yeah." Gavin seemed distracted. Probably getting his head back into business after their weekend of sensual escape. She wasn't going to be the kind of wife who demanded her husband's full attention twenty-four hours a day. She intended to be supportive and practical, and make sure she focused on her own business, as well.

A long, happy sigh escaped her lips. "I think I'll spend the day photographing couples." She shot him a smile. "They've always been my favorite subject. Now that I'm one half of a couple,

I'm even more excited about capturing the glow they share."

"Do they usually say yes when you ask?"

Bree thought for a moment. "Yes. The happy ones do. It's the unhappy ones who don't want their picture taken and recorded for all time."

"Then I hope you meet a lot of happy couples today."

"None of them will be as happy as me, that's for sure."

Bree sank back into the sheets after Gavin kissed her goodbye and left for work. Maybe after strolling the streets with her camera for a couple of hours, she'd head over to the lab to do some printing. There, in the dark, she could have a silly grin on her face all day and no one would care.

She glanced at the clock—almost nine! Advertising companies must get off to a leisurely start in the morning. Her dad was usually in the office by seven at the latest. But banking was different, and the stock market marched to an entirely different rhythm.

Speaking of rhythm, was that the phone? The sound of tingling music pulled her attention to the living room. She was sure he hadn't left the radio on. She climbed out of bed and pulled on her light robe. The music continued and she followed the sound to its source, where a green light flashed on a slim cordless phone on Gavin's desk.

Should she answer it? This was her house now, too. Still, it wasn't the house line. Gavin must have a separate one for business. She probably shouldn't answer it. For a start, she'd have to explain who she was, since hardly anyone even knew she and Gavin were married yet. Probably better to let the machine get it.

While she hesitated, Gavin's recorded message started to play, followed by a beep. She turned to leave the room, since it really was none of her business. The voice stopped her in her tracks.

"Morning, Gavin, or should I call you 'son'?" Her father's familiar gruff chuckle chilled her. Her dad was calling? Well, why not? She turned back to the phone to pick it up.

"The money's making its way into your account as I speak. One million big ones. I executed the wire transfer five minutes ago."

Rooted to the spot, Bree frowned at the phone. What on earth was he talking about? Dread crept over her, inch by cold, cruel inch.

"You're a fast mover, I'll give you that. I thought you'd have six months of courtship ahead of you. Bree's a prickly character where men are concerned, but I can see you swept her right off her size tens."

Her mouth fell open and her stomach dropped.

Her feet were only size nine. Not that it mattered.

Her throat closed and her heart started to pound.

"So now you can open your own business and support her in the style to which she's accustomed. I'm sure the two of you will be very happy." His chuckle sounded more like a malevolent cackle. Bree's hands shook, but she couldn't bring herself to grab the phone and ask what was going on.

She didn't need to. It was painfully obvious what had happened.

Her father had paid Gavin to marry her.

The click and dial tone snapped in the air like a fired bullet. The red light now flashing on the sleek phone told her this wasn't a figment of her imagination.

It was all fake. Every loving word, every kiss, every caress.

She shook her head as her brain rejected the idea. Hair tumbled into her eyes, and her breathing came heavy and ragged.

Money? Why did he want her money? He had a good job—didn't he? He must. She'd met all his coworkers. Still, there probably weren't too many people who couldn't use another million dollars.

One million dollars. So that was her value. Pretty high, all things considered.

A racking sob exploded through her. Why one million? Why not two? Or just two hundred thousand? Or twenty? Or a slice of pie from Stella's bakery?

She crumpled to the floor. It was hardwood, and her shins and elbows hit hard as she came down. The sharp pain didn't mean much, though, as agony soaked through her from the inside out.

How could you be so foolish as to think he wanted you just for yourself?

"Idiot!" She yelled the word aloud, and it bounced off the clean white walls.

She'd been suspicious at first. Wary. Prickly, as her father so astutely observed.

But her doubts and fears had capitulated under his volleys of kisses and flattering words. In less than two weeks he'd seduced her up the aisle, all for the promise of a nice, fat, financial reward.

Bree curled up into a ball on the hard, shiny floor. What now? She couldn't go home and face the father who'd sold her like an unfashionable antique he no longer wanted in his collection.

She certainly couldn't face her friends. She'd proudly called each one of them from their Sausalito hotel room to announce her newly married state. They'd mostly sounded so surprised—and why not? Obviously no one in their right mind would marry boring old Bree Kincannon unless there was a tempting added incentive.

Did everyone at his office know?

No. She drew in an unsteady breath. Unlikely. This must be a private deal between him and her father. It wasn't the kind of thing you'd want people getting wind of. Marrying a woman for money was…sleazy, to say the least, by today's standards.

Bree eased herself into a sitting position and hugged her legs. Likely she was the only person who knew, outside Gavin and her father, of course.

And right now it was her little dark and dirty secret.

Tears rolled over her cheeks and splashed in dark spots on her green silk robe. The one she'd bought to bring out the green in her…contact lenses.

A growl of fury slid between her teeth. She'd

let Elle doll her up and convince her she could attract a man like Gavin, when all along…

Was Elle in on it? The thought washed over her like an icy wave. She'd been an "instant friend," in a way that might make more savvy people suspicious. Had she been goaded by Gavin into turning his frumpy future bride into a woman who wouldn't embarrass him too much in company?

Bree bit her knuckle. It made sense. Gavin had introduced her to Elle and set the whole thing up. Bree snatched up the phone and was both angry and unsurprised to see Elle's name right there in the contacts list. She punched the button to dial and rose to her feet, fury flashing through her.

"Elle Linton."

"It's Bree." Her voice was dark and rasped.

"Bree?" Elle sounded surprised. "How are you?"

"How am I?" Bree turned and paced, trying not to let raw fury shut down her brain. "Let's see. I just found out that my new husband married me for money. How do you think I should be?"

"What?" Elle's voice rang with fake surprise.

"Don't pretend you weren't in on it. I know why you put so much effort into defrizzing my hair and finding me new clothes. Gavin put you up to it."

"I have no idea what you are talking about. Are you okay? You sound a little—"

"Crazy?" Bree snorted. "Yes. I believe you're right. And no, I don't think I'm okay. In fact, I've never felt less okay in my life."

"Hold on a minute, please."

Bree resisted the urge to slam down the phone. But of course she wouldn't hang up on someone—she was dependable old Bree and that would be rude.

"Sorry about that." Elle's breathless voice grated against her ear. "My desk is right outside Brock's office and not at all private. I'm in the ladies' room now. I still don't have a clue what you're talking about."

"Of course you do. I phoned you myself from Sausalito to tell you my happy news." The last two words dripped with venom.

"I know, and I'm thrilled for you both."

"Why, are you getting part of the money?" Ugly scenarios unfolded in Bree's mind.

"What money? Slow down, Bree, I don't know what you're talking about."

"The money my father paid Gavin to marry me."

The following silence sucked the last breath from Bree's lungs. Now that she'd said it aloud, to another person, the awful reality of what had just happened seemed literally unbearable. She paced into the bedroom, where the sheets were still warm and wrinkled from their most recent tryst.

"I don't believe it." Elle's shocked whisper came at last.

"You didn't know?"

"I swear it. I know Gavin from work, but not personally."

"Your number is programmed into his phone."

"I'm Brock's assistant. He calls me all the time to set up meetings."

"So you had no idea about any of this."

"Not the slightest clue, Bree."

"You've never lied to me about anything?"

A moment of silence followed. Elle's voice was subdued, quiet, when she spoke again. "Not about this. I was sure Gavin genuinely liked you. Where did you get this idea about the money?"

"Oh, just the message my own dear father left for him about the wire transfer."

"Bree, I'm so sorry. I had no idea."

"Why did you sound so hesitant when I asked if you'd lied?" Another pause made suspicion crackle through Bree's brain.

"I have a secret of my own." Elle's whisper startled her. "I wish I didn't because it's making lies part of my daily life." Silence hung in the air for a moment. "I'm having an affair with my boss."

"With Brock Maddox?" Bree didn't hide her surprise.

"Yes. I certainly never intended to, but things happened, and now…it's complicated. I wish I could tell you more, but it's better if I don't."

"I'll bet." Bree shook her head, trying to clear her tangled thoughts. What next?

"Do you love him?"

Elle's blunt question shocked her. "No."

"Not even a little?"

"I loved him madly until about four minutes ago. Does that make things clearer?"

"You can't switch love on and off. No one knows that better than me." Elle's voice was shadowed with regret. "You must still love him somewhere, underneath your anger and hurt."

"I'm sure I do. I'm dumb like that."

"Gavin's a good man. There's got to be something more to the story. Maybe this little discovery doesn't have to spoil everything. It could turn out to be a hiccup you can get past."

"That he took money to take me off my dad's hands? That's a lot to get past."

"Why don't you give him a chance?"

Could she? The possibility lit up Bree's brain like the lights on the Golden Gate Bridge. Could everything work out anyway? Could they live happily ever after and go whistling off into the sunset together?

Fresh tears pricked her eyelids and slid over her cheeks.

She swallowed hard. "Elle, you don't understand. This is what I've been so afraid of my whole life. I've always known men were only interested in me for the money I inherited from my mother. I fell so hard for Gavin because I was sure he was different. But he's no better than the rest. Worse, in fact."

"Maybe he really loves you, in spite of the money. Every time I saw him look at you, I could swear he had adoration written all over his face. I've never seen him like that before, and as you can imagine, he's never short of women flocking around him. I wouldn't say this if I didn't believe it, but I really think he loves you."

Bree cursed the way the possibility opened

inside her like a ray of fresh hope. "I guess there is a really tiny possibility that you could be right."

"He gets a very good salary and bonus—I should know, since I file all the records. He certainly wouldn't need to marry you for money. I think you should stick around and figure out what's going on before you throw away a good chance for happiness. Sometimes life is more complicated than we want it to be, but that doesn't mean it's not worth the trouble."

"I'm not sure I can philosophize right now, but I won't do anything rash." Bree frowned. "At the very least, I want to hear his side of the story."

"And maybe your relationship will end up stronger after you get through this."

"I very much doubt it, but I'll try to keep an open mind." Bree ran a hand through her tangled hair. "Don't tell anyone."

"I won't tell a soul. Trust me, due to some unfortunate circumstances, I've become very, very good at keeping secrets."

Bree put the phone back in its base. She carefully deleted the message from her father, and wiped her fingerprints from the shiny surface like a criminal, despite the fact that she was apparently the only innocent party in San Francisco.

When the phone rang again, she snatched it up, terrified of discovering yet more shocking secrets about her new husband.

Her husband. The word that had filled her with such joy a short while ago now filled her with sadness and regret.

It was the hotel in Sausalito on the phone. Their wedding photos were ready and had been mailed to them. Oh, joy. Pictures of her grinning like a lovesick fool on the arm of a man who swept her off her oversize feet just to fatten his wallet.

The big question was what to do when he came home tonight.

Seven

The sound of Gavin's key in the lock almost made Bree squeeze her eyes shut for a moment, but she didn't want to smudge her mascara. She'd just finished putting it on so she'd be sure not to cry.

"Hi, sweetheart." His warm, rich voice rang through the apartment.

"Hi," she called back, willing herself to sound bright and enthusiastic, as if she had no idea she'd been bartered for cold cash. "How was your day?"

"Pretty good." Gavin hung his suit jacket in the

closet and approached her, arms outstretched.
She tried not to steel herself against his hug.
Instead she stuck her arms out and approached
him with shaky knees. "How was yours?"

"Fine." One way to describe the worst day of
her life. "I made lasagna for dinner," she pro-
claimed, turning away before he could scruti-
nize her expression. She was still working on
keeping it serene.

"Mmm, fantastic. I was too busy to eat lunch
so it's lucky we didn't make plans."

"Something big going on at Maddox?"

"In a way." His voice had a funny tone to it
that made her turn around.

"Oh?"

"Me, leaving." A sheepish grin snuck across
Gavin's face. One that just a few hours ago she
would have found adorable.

She froze. "Leaving Maddox Communications?"
One million dollars was not enough to retire on.
Not in San Francisco, at least. Maybe he just
planned to kick back and live off her fortune?

She turned and marched to the kitchen to

check on the lasagna. The dish had helped get her focus off Gavin this afternoon. Might as well use it as a distraction now.

"You're shocked, aren't you?" Gavin followed her into the small galley kitchen. His physical presence filled the doorway and she fought a stray surge of desire.

"Well, yes. I thought you liked it there." She didn't look up. Instead she busied herself with taking the dish out of the oven.

"It was a good place to build my reputation. But now I'm ready to strike out on my own." He eased up beside her and slid his arms around her waist.

"Careful. This dish is hot." She tried to wriggle away from him, hating the way her stomach tingled under his fingers.

"Then don't look so irresistible. It's not fair to wear a dress like that and then not let me touch you."

Arousal rippled inside Bree at the touch of his hand on her hip. Curse him and this stupid dress. Another of the ones Elle had talked her into buying. Dark blue with a swirly skirt of clingy jersey.

"I just don't want to burn myself." *I've already been badly burned today.*

"All right, I'll set the table."

"I already did." She had everything planned and organized to perfection. She'd had plenty of time on her hands, after all, because the idea of photographing couples had quickly lost its charm. "Why don't you sit down? It's almost ready." She managed to keep her voice calm and even bright. Who knew she had such powers of deception?

She served the food with a smile. Gavin's admiring gaze took in her hard work primping this afternoon. She'd wanted to look good so he wouldn't know that inside she was in tiny pieces. "Why are you leaving Maddox Communications?"

Gavin's smile broadened, and took on a conspiratorial air. "To start my own company."

Bree swallowed as she sat down hard. Everything was becoming crystal clear. She called on an inner strength she hoped was in there somewhere. "What kind of company?"

"My own advertising shop. Boutique, top-notch creative, specializing in cutting-edge brands." The confident sparkle in his eye both aroused and infuriated her.

"Isn't that a risky endeavor? It must be hard to raise the money for a venture like that." She cocked her head, maintaining her placid demeanor.

Gavin's smile faded slightly, which gave her a moment of grim satisfaction. "Yes, no doubt it is, but I have years of experience now and I'm confident in my ability to make this endeavor succeed." He reached across the table and she let him take her hand and squeeze it. "With you by my side, there's no way I can fail."

His words rang hollow in the still air. Words that—if spoken yesterday—would have filled her with giddy pride. Today they sounded phony. A cliché. A lie.

Of course, in a way, he spoke the truth. It's hard to fail if the endeavor is underwritten by one of the most successful investors in San Francisco—who'd handed over the money as a reward for taking his daughter off his hands.

"So, are you bringing clients with you from Maddox?"

Gavin paused, fork hovering above his plate. "Much as I'd love to, I don't think that would be ethical."

"You wouldn't want to do anything unethical." Like, say, marry for money. "Much better to do things the honest, old-fashioned way." Like, say, marry for money. In the grand scheme of things, what he'd done wasn't all that outrageous. She'd bet nearly every single one of her ancestors had married for money. That would explain why there was so darn much of it in her bank account. Wait, was she trying to make excuses for him?

"Where do you plan to look for clients?"

"There are a couple who moved away from Maddox that I intend to pursue. And since I've put out the word I'm going out on my own, I've had some serious interest."

"Oh. How long have you been telling people you're starting your own company?" Hope bloomed in her chest. Perhaps this was something he'd been working on for some time that had nothing to do with her and her money. Maybe he was independently wealthy.

Maybe he really did love her.

Pathetic how she still shamelessly hoped for that.

"Just the last couple of days. I've been planning it for a long time but I was waiting for some things to come together."

"Oh." She stuck her fork into an innocent lettuce leaf. So much for her pathetic hopes. "How nice that they finally came together." She shot him a somewhat steely glance.

He didn't even notice—he just beamed at her. "It's the culmination of a lifelong dream. I've wanted my own company since I was a boy. At the time I had no idea it would be advertising, but that's what really gets my juices flowing."

Much to her chagrin, Gavin still got hers flowing. His excitement and enthusiasm were infectious. She almost wanted his company to be a big success just so she could enjoy that winning smile that lit up his chiseled features.

But she couldn't resist needling him a bit more.

"Juices are fun, but what about cash flow? Will things be tight while you get it off the ground?"

Gavin hesitated and looked at her as if surprised by her question. And really, why would an heiress ask the man she loved about money? Couldn't she just haul out some bags of gold bullion?

Then he leaned back in his chair, a satisfied look on his face. "I've got good start-up funds. Enough to rent a nice office space, pay good people and keep things going for at least six months even if it takes that long to land a client."

"Wow. You do have it well planned."

"It helps that I've got one of the best art directors in the country ready to come on board. Wait until you meet Tom, I know you'll like him. He does fine-art photography, too—collage mostly—and you'll recognize his work as soon as you see it. He's going to bring a couple of key people from the agency he's at now."

"I bet they won't be too happy."

Gavin shrugged. "Advertising is a bit of a dog-eat-dog world. Agencies form, merge, gain clients, lose clients. It's all part of the business. You're only as good as your biggest client."

"And who do you hope to snag as your biggest client?"

Gavin cocked his head and gave her a cheeky glance that tickled her insides. "You'll laugh if I tell you."

"I could use a good laugh."

He hesitated a moment. "No. Let me surprise you when I really do win them."

"Great. I love surprises." He didn't seem to notice the slight edge of sarcasm that crept into her voice. How could he string her along like this? How could he sit there and eat dinner so casually, when their whole marriage was a farce? Did he really intend to spend the rest of his life with her, or was she a temporary fund-raising measure until he got his company off the ground?

Then he'd probably kick her to the curb and bring in a slender blonde who'd look better on his arm at the awards ceremonies.

No doubt that's exactly what he had in mind. He wasn't going to spend the rest of his life saddled with a dumpy nobody. Not once he really had his own money and didn't need hers.

She shoved a bite of lasagna into her mouth, to stem the flood of angry words to her tongue. Part of her wanted to let him have it—tell him she knew and how disgusted she was that he'd tricked her into marrying him. For a single sharp instant she fantasized about standing up now and yelling right at him. Ending everything, right now, and watching his startled reaction.

But common sense got the better of her. She couldn't bear to spew out all her hurt and shame. That would only give him power over her. He'd probably tell her she was all wrong and that he truly loved her and, sucker that she was, she'd probably believe him.

No. She had a better plan. Play him at his own game.

She'd make him think everything was working out perfectly. His happy little wife was sitting at home tinkering with her photos while he took the world by storm. She'd play along, encourage and support him, pretend to love and adore him the way he obviously expected.

Then, just when he was least prepared, she'd tell him she knew the truth and boot him out of her life.

"Great lasagna, Bree."

"Thanks." She forced a wide smile. "I like it with béchamel sauce instead of ricotta. More authentic, I think."

"I can't believe that on top of everything else you're an amazing cook, too."

"It's nothing. I enjoy cooking. You should tell me all your favorite meals so I can make them for you." Maybe that would make him truly fall in love with her. Food was supposed to be the way to a man's heart. After money, of course.

Revenge would be sweet if he did actually fall for her before she revealed her secret.

"I love seafood." Gavin's gray eyes sparkled. "And barbecue. We'll have to set a grill up on the balcony. I scorch some mean shrimp."

"Sounds delicious. Perhaps when we buy our house we can set up an outdoor dining room." She smiled sweetly.

"I love that idea. I've been too lazy to entertain living here on my own. I usually go out. But when we have a real home, we'll have to have friends over often." He leaned forward, obviously enjoying his vision of their future.

It did sound fun. Friends gathered for a casual, outdoor meal. What a shame none of it was real. They were both just playing along, pretending, maintaining a charade.

"This salad dressing is sensational." He sucked a trace of the rich concoction off his fork, a gesture that caused an unpleasant sizzle deep inside her.

How could you still be attracted to him?

"It's the olive oil. I buy it fresh in Sonoma from an old guy there who has the most amazing orchard. Nothing tastes like it."

"We'll have to go there together."

"Absolutely."

"Still, it's not just the oil, it's the blend of spices. You have a real talent."

"Oh, I have all kinds of hidden talents." She tossed the curls she'd nurtured into shiny ringlets and smiled coyly. "You have no idea." She certainly was surprised that she'd managed to keep her cool so far. Maybe she did have undiscovered facets that this whole disastrous misadventure would polish to a shine.

Like a capacity to exact the perfect revenge on the man who'd made her worst nightmare come true.

That night, when Gavin's hands found her body under the covers, she yielded to his touch. It wasn't hard. In fact, it would have been almost impossible not to. Desire still throbbed inside her like an incurable ache. A day ago she might have called it love, or something foolish like that, but now she recognized it for the pure physical urge it was.

She wrapped her arms around his sturdy torso and let herself enjoy the sweet warmth of his skin against hers. She'd been so very lonely today. Would it hurt to enjoy sex before she went back to hating him?

As they moved together she let herself enjoy the sensation as a dance—pleasure that crept through every inch of her. Didn't people do this all the time and mean nothing by it?

He'd have been suspicious if she pushed him away. Not that she even had the willpower to do that.

When he kissed her on the mouth, she found herself kissing back with passion, unable to stop. Her climax pounded through her, making her clutch him tighter.

It doesn't mean anything, her mind protested, over the louder drumbeat of her blood. *You'll forget him.*

She would try, anyway.

* * *

Gavin donned his best power suit for a day of key meetings. For some reason, being married gave him an extra edge of stability—almost like a foundation—that made it easy to go out and take on the world. He'd noticed Bree seemed a little nervous lately—on edge, even. Perhaps she was worried about him stepping out on his own. Hopefully he'd soon be able to reassure her by obtaining clients.

Of course he could reassure her right now by mentioning that he had ample start-up funds, but he wasn't quite sure how she'd react to his deal with her father.

Guilt trickled through him like acid. He wished he could have pulled this off without the money, but you couldn't start a business without capital.

He'd make it up to her by being a devoted husband.

He kissed Bree after eating the delicious breakfast of bacon, eggs and fresh rolls that she'd made him. For some reason, she was dressed to

the nines, in a pretty green dress that accentu-
ated her curves. "You look beautiful, as always.
I'll see you at the party tonight."

She cocked her head, her curls falling over
one shoulder. "What party?"

"I thought I told you. There's a big shindig
tonight to celebrate winning the new Reynolds
Automotive account."

A shadow crossed her face. "No, you didn't
say a word."

"Hmm. I wasn't sure quite how Brock would
react to the news of me leaving. Maybe I half
thought he'd have tossed me out on my ear by
now."

"I'm surprised he hasn't." She cocked a
brow.

"He said he trusts me. They've had some
strange things going on at the agency lately,
a mole of sorts, leaking information to a rival
agency, and I've been helping him try to solve
the problems it's caused. I also helped to win the
Reynolds account, so he wants me to do some
more work on that before I go."

"Nice to have a boss who thinks so highly of you." Gavin glanced up. He almost thought he heard a note of sarcasm in Bree's voice. No. It couldn't be. Her lovely smile lit up the room.

"Yeah. I'm sure some people think I'm crazy to leave, but everything reaches its natural limit eventually."

"Even a marriage?" She looked him directly in the eye in a way that spiked his blood pressure slightly. Maybe all the changes were making her feel insecure.

He quirked a smile. "'Till death us do part.' That's the only natural limit I can see." He kissed her soft cheek. Did she stiffen slightly as he hugged her?

It was a shame he had to leave right away. He had a breakfast meeting with the marketing director of Argos Shoes, an account he'd give almost anything to win. He was even prepared to eat breakfast again, since he hadn't wanted to disappoint Bree by turning down the fantastic meal she'd prepared to surprise him.

"Death, yes, I suppose you're right." Her green

eyes surveyed him with a slightly unsettling look. "Hopefully that's a ways off, but I suppose you never know."

"You're in a rather grim mood this morning."

She shrugged, which had the dangerous effect of pulling the green fabric tighter over her spectacular breasts. Gavin shoved down a surge of desire welling inside him. "I'd better get out of here before I get distracted and miss my meetings. Bye, my love."

He kissed her and headed for the elevator. If things went well today, his new agency would be off to a flying start, and he'd be able to put Bree's fears to rest.

Bree sagged against the door after it closed behind Gavin. She hadn't hidden her emotions too well this morning. She'd donned the full makeup and the fancy dress, preparing a good breakfast and smiling like a store mannequin, but she couldn't seem to hide the hurt and fear roiling just below her manicured surface.

Making love—no, having sex—last night hadn't helped. The intimacy only reminded her of everything she'd lose when she pushed Gavin out of her life. She'd been happy alone because she'd never known anything different. Now she'd be agonizingly aware of all the pleasures of couplehood she'd be missing out on.

Ali brushed up against her legs. "I know, Princess, it's time for your shot. You're still my first love. I shouldn't have asked for more." Her stately fifteen-year-old cat paused, as if agreeing. "And at least I'll still have you and Faith when he's gone." She reached down and stroked Ali's soft back. "That will be more than enough."

She kicked off the stupid heels she'd put on to clack around the apartment as Little Mrs. Perfect. How had she let herself get duped into this? And now she had to put on the "perfect wife" act at a party with all his friends and co-workers? She wanted to cry.

Heck, maybe she would go ahead and have a cry. It couldn't hurt. That way she could get it out of her system and grin like a loon all night on the arm of the lying Gavin Spencer.

After Bree's odd behavior that morning, Gavin decided to go home and pick her up so they could arrive at the party together. He worried that she felt overwhelmed by her new life, and he felt guilty for announcing his dramatic career change so soon after their wedding. He probably should have given her a bit more time to get comfortable. And given that some of his coworkers were a bit testy about his announcement, he decided it might be better if they went to the party together so she didn't show up and get grilled by anyone before he got there.

"You look gorgeous, as usual." He had to pause for a moment, just to take in the vision of Bree standing in their apartment door. Her ankle-length dress, covered in tiny black-and-white stripes, flowed over her curves like water down a waterfall.

"Thanks. I did some shopping today." Her green eyes glittered hard as she gazed at him.

Or possibly he was just imagining it. All the upheaval in his professional life must be making him testy. Bree seemed taller than usual, and a glance down confirmed that she wore sleek black-and-white pumps that added about three inches to her already impressive height. "Lucky I'm over six feet or I'd be standing in your shadow." He grinned.

She smiled tightly. "Now that I'm married, I don't have to worry that no one will dance with me because I'm too tall."

"An excellent point." She did look gorgeous. Her height served only to emphasize her Greek-goddess good looks, especially with her magnificent ringlets cascading over her shoulders. She must have spent hours getting ready.

Now that he thought about it, she'd been dressed to the nines even for their dinner at home last night. "You don't have to look breathtaking every minute, you know. It's okay to relax and wear whatever feels comfortable."

She cocked her head, which sent her curls tumbling over one breast. "Do you think I should wear that dress I had on when we met?"

He grinned. "Okay, maybe not that one. But I don't want you thinking you have to dress up all the time."

"Not a problem. I just dress how I like." She lifted her chin, tall and proud.

"As long as it's for your own pleasure, it's all good with me." Who wouldn't want a woman who looked as fantastic as this? He couldn't understand why no one had snatched her up before him. Her father must be nuts to think she needed his help in finding a husband.

He'd transferred the money, though. Gavin had seen it in the new account he'd opened just for this purpose. One million dollars—seven fat figures—right there on the screen of the computer under his name. Could life get any better than this?

He extended his arm to Bree, who threaded hers elegantly through it. "Let's go take the world by storm."

The Iron Grille restaurant on the first floor of

the agency building throbbed with music, and waiters in white tie swirled through the crowd with trays of hors d'oeuvres.

"Oh, Gavin!" He grimaced at the site of nutty Marissa barreling toward him on her high heels, stringy blonde hair flying. He certainly wouldn't miss her. "Go on, tell me in secret. Which clients are you stealing, darling?"

"Marissa, I believe you've met my wife, Bree."

Marissa glanced at Bree, managing to look down on her, despite the fact that Bree was several inches taller. "Congratulations on your big catch, darling." Then she turned her evil gaze back to Gavin. "Or should I be congratulating you, sweetheart? I hear Bree's from old money."

Bree's mouth dropped open. Even he was rendered speechless. "Marissa, you're lucky you're a talented logo designer, or no one would put up with you."

"So true!" She grinned. "But come on, who

are you stealing? Or are you the infamous mole everyone's been hunting for all year?"

He was in danger of losing his cool if he didn't get away from this woman. "Bree, let's go find a drink. I'm starting to need one." Bree looked panicked—not surprising. Marissa had that effect on people.

"Oh, go on and get your drink, handsome." Marissa waved heavily ringed fingers at him. "Logan doesn't think you're the mole anyway. And he would know."

The mention of his second least favorite Maddox employee stopped Gavin in his tracks. "Logan? What does he have to do with anything?"

"Didn't you know?" She pursed her lips with thinly concealed glee. "He's not an account executive at all. He's a private detective."

"That explains a few things about his performance." Gavin frowned. "Did Brock hire him to find the source of the leaks?" He couldn't believe he had to learn this from Marissa. Why hadn't Brock himself told him?

"You betcha, babe. And from your adorable surprise, I can see he didn't trust you with that information. You must have been on his list of suspects." She shot Bree a supercilious smile. "You watch out for this one, darling. There's more to him than meets the eye." She winked at him. "Though what meets the eye isn't half-bad."

Then she turned on her heels and vanished into the crowd.

Bree stood staring after her.

"Brock should get rid of her. A loose cannon like that is a danger to the company."

"So, apparently, is a mole. What did she mean by that?" Bree wasn't smiling or looking amused.

"Someone's been stealing company secrets and leaking them to the competition. It's been going on for a few months, and no one has any idea who it is."

"It sounds like Brock thought it might be you." Worry—or was it suspicion?—danced in

Bree's green eyes. A nasty feeling crept through Gavin.

"I suppose he had to suspect everyone, though I assure you I'd rather die than betray my employer."

Bree simply cocked her head and narrowed her eyes. "I wonder if he thinks your leaving is a betrayal."

"No. People come and go in this business all the time. Par for the course."

Bree simply closed her lips in a tight smile. Did she really think he was capable of undermining the company? What was going on with her? "I think we both need some wine. Or maybe champagne."

"I couldn't agree more."

Gavin spent the rest of the party reassuring people that he had no intention of stealing Maddox clients for his new company. Some were surprised he was even there. Everyone was whispering about Logan Emerson being a private detective, but no one knew if he'd uncovered the spy.

At one point, Elle grabbed Bree by the hand and whisked her away. She explained that they were going out for some girl talk, and she'd escort Bree home. This was rather a relief for Gavin, since Bree seemed unusually tense. On top of the drama of his own departure and the hushed mutterings about the in-house traitor, the party was unusually exhausting. After only half an hour, he ducked out and headed upstairs into the Maddox offices to box up the last of his stuff. He was more than ready to leave Maddox Communications behind and start fresh.

He grinned at the weary security guard as he got off the elevator on the sixth floor. "Is the place locked? I might need you to let me in. I handed in my key."

"Mr. Maddox told me you'd be coming by. He's inside himself."

"Brock is in the office?" Odd. Gavin had noticed he wasn't at the party.

"Been there all evening. Sent out for dinner a while back, but told me to make sure he wasn't disturbed by anyone except you. Sent out for a bottle of whiskey, too." The elderly security guard raised his wiry brows.

Gavin frowned. What was going on? He couldn't take much more of this intrigue. He pushed into the open offices. "Brock?"

"Back here." His boss's voice was gruff. "Come on in."

He crossed the dark office to the light pooling out of Brock's door. Tension hung in the air like day-old cigar smoke. Inside the office, Brock sat in his big, leather chair behind the antique desk, his face uncharacteristically haggard.

"I didn't know my leaving was going to have such a dramatic effect on you," Gavin quipped.

"Trust me, you're the least of my problems."

"You do know I'm not the spy, don't you?"

Brock rubbed a hand over his face. "Believe me, it would be easier if you were."

Gavin strode across the room and pulled up a chair. "You know who it is?"

Brock drew in a deep breath. "Sure do. The gumshoe I hired finally found irrefutable evidence." An odd expression flickered across his face.

"The suspense is killing me."

"It's Elle."

Gavin frowned. "Your assistant?"

"Do you know any other Elles?"

"But she was at the party just now, downstairs. Bree left with her." Panic gripped his heart. Exactly what was going on here?

"I haven't yet told her that I know."

"Why not?"

"We're lovers." Brock picked up a crystal tumbler and took a hearty draught of the gold liquid.

Gavin sank back in his chair. "Holy—"

"What surprises you more—the fact that I'm having an affair with my assistant or the fact that she's a corporate spy?" He lifted a black brow and leveled his piercing blue gaze at Gavin.

"But why?"

"I'll give you the benefit of the doubt and assume you're asking why she was spying.

You won't believe this. She's Athos Koteas's granddaughter."

Athos Koteas ran Golden Gate Promotions, Maddox's long-time rival on the San Francisco ad scene. The enmity dated back decades and had intensified lately, since competition for good clients was tighter than ever. "You really think they sent her here to sabotage your business?"

"I know it. And I've been fool enough to give her access to all our files, even the most confidential, as well as my bed. She's been undermining our operations and giving Golden Gate a top crack at all our clients for months."

Gavin blew out a long, hard breath. "I assume you're going to fire her."

"Right now I don't know what the hell to do." His blue eyes glittered with pain. "You think you know someone, and then…" He rubbed a hand over his brow.

A curse fell from Gavin's lips. "You know, I introduced Elle to Bree. They've even spent time together on the weekends. Now I'm worried she may have tricked Bree into something."

That might explain why Bree looked so tense earlier.

"I have no idea what kind of damage she's done, and all the while I thought..." Brock growled. "I don't know what I thought. Women. You'd better watch out, Gavin. You never quite know what's going on in their minds."

Eight

Bree was pacing the apartment when Gavin arrived home shortly before midnight. Elle had tried to console her and convince her that Gavin was worth a second chance, but right now she was in too much pain to do anything but try to get through the night.

"Hi, Bree." Gavin closed the door behind him. Tall and majestic in his dark suit, he looked as strikingly handsome as ever. Was that fair?

"Hi, Gavin." Her voice cracked slightly, so she forced a bright smile. "How was the rest of the party?"

He frowned. "Very interesting. What exactly did you and Elle talk about after you left?"

She froze. Had Elle told Gavin that she knew about his deal with her father?

"I ask because Brock has discovered that Elle is the spy at Maddox." He threw his jacket down on a chair and marched into the room.

"What?" Bree's head spun. The neat puzzle of her new life was breaking apart and she no longer had all the pieces.

"Brock had a private detective working in-house. He's been tracking and tailing the staff for weeks, undercover as an account executive. A very bad account executive, I might add. I kept wondering why Brock didn't fire him." He pulled a soda from the fridge and popped it open. "Want one?"

"No," she managed. "Elle is a crook?" Her voice came out high and squeaky.

"I don't know if she's broken any laws, but she's certainly broken Brock's trust."

"But they're…" She felt her face heat. Maybe

Gavin didn't know about Elle's intimate relationship with Brock.

"Having an affair. He told me that, too. Maybe she planned it that way so he'd be less likely to suspect her."

Bree found herself staggering backward to the sofa where she sat down heavily. Wearing high heels all the time was a bad idea when the world kept tilting beneath you. She blinked, conscious of the green contact lenses she never took out. It was hard work being Little Mrs. Perfect.

Especially when everyone you liked and trusted turned out to have an ulterior motive.

Gavin walked toward her. "Did she extract any information from you?"

"Elle?" Bree racked her brain. "I don't think so. What kind of information might she have wanted?"

"About the Maddox accounts, I imagine."

"I don't know anything about them. How would I?"

He turned and paced across the room. "Could be she wants information about my new agency.

I'm going to be more competition for Golden Gate. Did she ask about my plans?"

"She didn't, but even if she had, I don't know anything about them, either." There was a trace of bitterness in her voice. He hadn't mentioned his big plans to her until after he'd secured the funding for them by marrying her.

"True." He shoved a hand through his dark hair, and she cursed the sting of arousal that heated her belly. "What kinds of things did you talk about?"

"Girl stuff." *You.* "Nothing about business at all."

"I suppose that's something." He took a swig of his soda. "Let's put all this intrigue behind us and move on to more important things."

Bree sat stiffly, wondering what they would be.

"First of all, we haven't kissed since I came in the door." He rose from the chair and before she could protest he'd picked her up off the sofa, whirled her around and planted a big, hot kiss on her lips that turned her insides upside down.

When he pulled back he was grinning. Breathless, heart pounding, Bree struggled to be put down. How could she still be aroused by him? Her nipples tightened and heat cascaded over her, settling between her thighs. She felt breathless and unsteady.

All because of a man who didn't care one bit about her.

He set her down gently on her precarious heels. "The really good news is that I have my first client. I got the call while I was at the party. Crieff Jewelers wants me to put together a campaign for them, to run in the top glossies."

"That's fantastic!" Bree couldn't help the expression of genuine glee. How could she be happy for him after all she'd learned? "You've worked hard for it." Marrying a virtual stranger was pretty hard work, after all.

"And I'd like you to be the photographer."

Her heart leapt. "You're kidding."

"Not even a little bit. I've seen your work and you're a top-notch talent."

Bree blinked. Did he really admire her

photography, or was that just part of the act? Surely he wouldn't risk his first real client if he didn't think her work was up to scratch.

Unless there wasn't a real client and this was just a ruse to butter her up.

Crieff Jewelers, though. They were probably the most highbrow and expensive jeweler in the entire Bay area. The kind of place her dad would go for some custom cufflinks. And they were known for particularly sleek and eye-catching ad campaigns. Ideas and imagery began to dance in her mind.

But did Gavin really want her work, or just some free photos? She decided to put him to the test. "I'm a professional photographer. You'd have to pay me." She shot him an arch smile.

Gavin looked slightly taken aback, but he took her hands and squeezed them. "Of course you'll be paid. Ten thousand for the day's shoot, an additional thousand for each hour after five. It's the top rate at Maddox." He actually looked kind of anxious, as if he really wanted her to say yes.

"Then I'll do it." A smile flooded her face.

How could she not be excited about an opportunity like this? It would be fun, however it came about. Something new and unexpected to add to her portfolio, and who knows, maybe a whole new direction for her budding photography career.

Gavin planted a soft kiss on her mouth that intensified the rush of feelings flooding through her. "We're a great team, babe."

Her heart sank. They were only a team as long as she could keep up this pretense of a happy marriage. Sooner or later the façade of wedded bliss would come crumbling down, and she had no idea how she'd extricate herself from that wreckage. His smile would certainly fade when she caused an embarrassing scandal asking for a divorce—if you even needed one after so little time. He wouldn't pay her fee, either, after her ruthless father demanded his money back.

Bree jumped up from the table and ran for the bathroom as tears threatened. The worst part was, she dreaded the prospect of hurting him, of crushing his dreams the way he'd destroyed hers. She blotted her mascara with a tissue and sucked in a deep breath. *You're supposed to be getting revenge, remember?*

Bree beamed with excitement as Gavin welcomed the clients to the full-service photo studio they'd hired for the day. The team from Crieff, a man and a woman, were young and hip. They'd e-mailed Bree snapshots of some of the pieces, and she'd sent back sketches of ideas, which they'd loved. Two sleek models sat at the other end of the studio, ready to wear the gems against an assortment of clingy black clothes Bree had borrowed from her new favorite boutique. The store had been happy to help, possibly because Bree had bought armfuls of clothing from them to augment her new image.

Gavin's new assistant passed around mint tea and freshly made lemonade, as well as coffee while they chatted about Bree's ideas. She felt oddly relaxed and professional. Having Gavin by her side, confident and beaming, didn't hurt. Why did he have to be so darned…happy?

Then again, why wouldn't he be? His big dream was coming true. It was hard not to share his exhilaration—she had to keep reminding herself she was just a pawn in his game.

She styled the models with the help of a professional hair stylist and a makeup artist, and took shot after shot. The results were fantastic—exactly what she hoped for—especially some rather arty black-and-white ones she talked them into, using real film instead of digital for a film-noir effect.

"She's a genius. Where did you find her?" The man from Crieff slapped Gavin on the back as they looked at some proofs on a laptop.

"I'm a very lucky man. She's my wife." He grinned at Bree. She glowed for a moment before remembering why she was his wife—so he could be here, getting slapped on the back by clients.

It would probably be better if she'd never found out. Right now she'd be glowing with happiness while having the time of her life, working a professional photography job with the love of her life by her side.

Revenge be damned. She couldn't live this lie any longer. It was time to tell Gavin she knew the truth.

"They loved the shots!" Gavin exclaimed, not for the first time, as they marched along Market Street after the shoot. Warm sunset tones lit up the old stone facades of the buildings.

"Yep. They seemed pretty happy." A contented smile snuck across her face.

"You really should consider a career in advertising photography." He squeezed her. They were walking along with their arms around each other, presenting a façade of wedded bliss for all to see.

"Maybe I will." *Just not with you.*

"You looked as if you were really enjoying the challenge. You did a fantastic job saying just the right thing to the models to get the look right. That's not easy, you know."

"It was fun. I could see myself doing some

magazine work." She tossed her curls. She really could! Despite its downside, this episode with Gavin had boosted her confidence in herself and her capabilities.

"I think this calls for a big celebration dinner, so I made reservations at my new favorite restaurant, Iago's." Iago's was an especially fancy dining spot that Bree had heard her father talk about.

"Why not? Sounds like the perfect spot for a big-shot advertising company president to eat."

"That's what I'm thinking." Gavin's warm grin almost—almost—melted her resolve. Then she let the words of that overheard message replay in her head. *One million big ones.* That's what their whole "romance" was really about.

It was time to put her plan into action, which required a few organizational steps. "I need to go home and change."

"That's okay, we've got forty-five minutes. I figured you'd want to freshen up. You're such a stylish dresser." His gray eyes drifted over the simple black pantsuit she'd worn.

Bree Kincannon, a stylish dresser. She had been, lately. How funny.

Panic snuck through her as she realized she needed him out of the house so she could pack her things and get the cats into their crates. "Gavin, would you do me a huge favor and pick up a box of prints from my dad's house while I get changed?" That would take a good forty-five minutes, and he wouldn't have time to come home. "Give me the address of the restaurant. I'll meet you there."

"Sure. Here it is." He fished a sleek black matchbox out of his pocket, and handed it to her. She glanced at the address. Good, she could park in the public lot nearby.

She drew in a deep breath to steady her nerves. "It's a big blue plastic box to the left of my desk. I can't believe I forgot it." She didn't really need the box—her collection of prints that didn't quite make the cut—but this was her chance to get some time alone. To plan her escape. Heck, maybe he'd even run into her dad and they could have a nice round of congratulations….

Right before she blew their nasty little plot out of the water.

Gavin escorted her into the city's most exclusive new restaurant. Well-heeled diners, many in elegant evening clothes, sat at tables decorated with fresh flowers. Golden light shone through a wall of windows with a lovely view over the water. His hand on her lower back guided her through the forest of floor length tablecloths to the table with the best view of all, on a tiny balcony jutting out toward the bay.

"You must know people to get this table," she whispered.

"Only the best for my beautiful bride."

Bree's stomach clenched. This atmosphere of hushed refinement was hardly the place to make a scene. Maybe she'd better wait until they got home before she confronted him.

No, she had the whole thing planned. Her car was packed and her cats sitting quietly in their crates, with the windows cracked to give them air. She had a two-week supply of Ali's medicine and Faith's special food.

Terror unfurled inside her. Could she really do this? Just take off?

She drew in a deep, shaky breath, which caused her breasts to swell in the oh-so-stylish green dress she'd donned for the occasion. She wanted Gavin to remember her looking good, right before she brought the guillotine down on all his neat plans.

Gavin pulled back her seat, the perfect gentleman as always. She eased herself into it and spread the fine linen napkin on her lap. The waiter poured champagne and described the creative dishes on special.

"You were fantastic today." Gavin rested a warm gaze on her face. If she hadn't known better she'd think it was genuine admiration. "You had such an easy way with the clients. Some people are very nervous around them."

"I was trained from an early age." The heiress thing. She'd learned to converse comfortably with everyone from royalty to the staff, while mastering the alphabet. "Comes in handy sometimes."

"And you were so calm, even though we all knew we had only one day for the shoot."

"I knew we'd get it done."

"I wish there were more photographers like you around." He grinned and raised his glass. Why did he have to be so gorgeous? The smile sneaking across her mouth should be fake, but it wasn't. She just couldn't help it. Gavin was infuriatingly likeable.

"Why, so you could hire them instead of me?" She raised a brow and winked.

"Why do that, when I can keep it all in the family?" He reached across the table and she gave him her hand. "Isn't it just too perfect?"

"Yes, it's just too perfect." She struggled to keep emotion out of her voice.

Gavin's eyes sparkled with excitement about his new venture, not passion for her. Everything was too neat and pretty and nice to be real.

Because, of course, it wasn't.

The waiter served the artfully prepared appetizers. Bree picked up her fork, but her stomach was not interested in food and anxiety boiled in her gut.

Now. Tell him now.

But how could she, when he beamed with such pure happiness? She was usually the one to smooth everything over and soothe the proverbial troubled waters. She preferred to ease hurt feelings and make everyone feel better—even at her own expense. She was good old Bree, who you could always count on in a crunch.

Or at least she used to be.

Before dreams she'd never known she had all came true—and then fell apart within a week in the most cruel and hurtful way possible. Pain stabbed her chest, goading her into action.

She looked up from her sautéed shrimp. "Gavin, when exactly did you know you'd fallen in love with me?"

A tiny frown appeared on his forehead. "Hmm, what an interesting question."

"Was it when you first saw me, in that frumpy

gray dress with no makeup and my wild-haystack hair?" She maintained a pleasant expression. "When I was so nervous I could hardly speak?"

He cocked his head. "No, I don't think it was right then."

"So why did you ask me to dance?"

"Why not?"

"Well—" she swallowed "—it's just that men usually only ask me to dance when they're interested in my money." She leveled a serious gaze at him. "I'm used to that. Somehow it all seemed different with you."

"Because it was different with me. I'm attracted to you, not your wealth." He took a sip of champagne. For a split second she thought she saw a flicker of unease cross his chiseled features. "I'm attracted to you for who you are."

Hurt welled inside Bree. How could he maintain a pleasant expression while telling such outright lies?

"But you were more attracted to me once I... changed my image."

"I wouldn't say that." A cute, rueful grin tugged at his mouth. "Okay, maybe I would. You really are a knockout when you dress the part, Bree."

"I know that now. Though I really should give Elle all the credit. She's the one who transformed me from a frizzy-haired wallflower into the belle of the ball. Quite the fairy godmother, really. And I even got the handsome prince in the end, too."

Gavin frowned. "Elle transformed you? What is she up to? Ever since Brock told me she's the spy, I know there's far more to her than meets the eye. You should be careful around her. Who knows what she was trying to get out of you. You didn't give her any financial information, did you?"

"Of course not." *No, we wouldn't want her getting her hands on the money you want for yourself.* Tears welled inside her, but she held them back. Not yet. There'd be plenty of time for crying later. "But I did like her. And trust her. I'm a trusting person, or at least I used to be." Her voice cracked.

"She's broken your trust?"

Bree drew in a slow, steady breath. "Not her. Someone else."

Gavin frowned. "Who?" He leaned forward. "Just tell me and I'll go sort them out. I don't want anyone hurting your feelings." His gray eyes fixed on her face with probing intensity.

"You."

The single word fell from her lips and hung in the air for a moment.

Gavin's frown deepened. "I don't under-stand."

"No? Maybe you'd understand if I mentioned a certain number with six zeros."

He put his fork down on the tablecloth, still staring straight at her, and shoved a hand through his dark hair.

"I overheard a message my father left on your machine, thanking you for taking me off his hands—for a sizeable price, of course, since obviously no one would want to be stuck with me for nothing." Her voice rattled with the tears that wanted to come, but she forced herself to stay steady.

"He offered to help me start my own business. It's a simple investment on his part." He had the decency to look alarmed.

"Don't lie to me." She raised her voice. "I heard what he said. He was surprised you managed to seduce me into it so quickly. Usually I'm more sensible than that." She pulled her wedding and engagement rings from her finger, struggling to get them over her knuckle. "I've had plenty of men sniffing around my money and pretending to like me, so usually I can spot them a mile off. You were different, though. Far better looking, for one thing."

She took a final glance at his fine, handsome face. The kind of face she could have happily photographed and kissed for a lifetime—if it weren't the face of a scheming traitor.

"I am different. I'm not interested in your money."

"You took it, though, didn't you?"

"Your father's money." His voice was gruff. "Yes, I took it. Because I wanted to start my own business. I'd been waiting a long time and suffered some financial setbacks that made it impossible until your father offered me the chance—"

"To take advantage of a going-out-of-business sale on his spinster daughter." She blinked back tears. "Now I know why you were in such a rush to get married. Why you didn't want a long engagement with an announcement in the papers, or even a real wedding. None of that was important to you because it wasn't about our marriage—or us—at all. It was all about money. Well, I'm not here to be given away, even with a million dollars." Her voice rang out, shattering the hushed refinement of the exclusive restaurant as she rose to her feet and threw the rings at him. They bounced across the tablecloth and disappeared as her chair crashed to the wood floor.

She rushed for the door, bumping into a table on the way and almost dragging the tablecloth with her, unsteady in her high heels. Panting, tears now running down her cheeks, she shoved her way out the door and ran for the fire stairs, clattering down until she reached street level.

Gavin wasn't behind her. Had she hoped he'd rush after her, try to convince her it was all a big mistake? She should have known better.

Their fairy-tale romance was a farce and the broken pieces of her dreams could never be put back together again.

It was almost completely dark when she reached the street, and she stayed in the shadows away from the streetlamps until she got to her car, parked two blocks away. Her hands shook as she fumbled in her bag for the keys, but Ali and Faith greeted her with mewing and purrs. "I'm here, ladies. We're making our escape together."

She settled into the cold leather seat and started the engine. Something tight gripped her heart as she pulled out into the late rush-hour traffic and headed for the freeway.

It was over.

With any luck, she'd never see Gavin again. Maybe one day she'd even forget him.

No. She'd never forget him. How could she forget someone who had tricked her into pledging her whole life to him?

How could she forget the firm warmth of his arms around her? The powerful touch of his fingers on her skin, or the soft enticement of his kiss?

"Damn him!" She pounded her fist on the wheel. Why did he have to introduce her to pleasures she'd never dared hope for? He should pay for that.

He would. She knew he would. Even if there wasn't a big scandal.

Her father would be sure to ask for the money back. He wasn't going to pay a million dollars for a marriage that had lasted less than a month. Elliott Kincannon was far too shrewd an investor for that.

No. Gavin would have to pay it all back, his business would fold and soon he'd be begging Brock Maddox to take him back.

Guilt speared through her, and she cursed herself for it. Deep down she still wanted him to succeed and be happy. And why not? That's the kind of sucker she was.

She let out a howl of anguish, spilling her pain into the night air.

What a fool she'd been, to think someone could love her for herself.

Nine

Gavin's gaze followed the rings as they bounced across the tablecloth, onto the floor. Slightly dazed, he ducked down and groped on the floor to retrieve them. Bree's angry words rattled in his skull.

Yes—there it was—the triple diamond his grandmother had left him. He palmed it and sat up, relieved. "Bree—"

She'd gone. He scanned the room, but she seemed to have vanished into the understated decor. He stood, ring still clutched in his hand.

"Can I help you, sir?" A waiter hurried over.

"Where did she go?"

"Your companion?"

"Yes!" Glancing about, he saw only the faces of strangers.

"I'm afraid I didn't see." He leaned closer. "Perhaps she's in the ladies'."

Gavin frowned. "I don't think so. I'd better pay the check." Urgency prickled under his skin.

"The entrées won't be a minute, sir."

"No, but…I have to go." People were staring. He reached into his pocket and pulled out three fifties. Hopefully that would cover it.

Damn, the other ring. He got down on the floor and peered around at the polished wood. The engraved gold band inscribed with both their initials sat quietly near a table leg. He snatched it up and pocketed it before climbing to his feet.

"Is there a problem, sir?" The maître d' approached, concern written on his dark brow.

"No problem at all. Just that something's come up." He cleared his throat. He could feel the curious stares and hear the whispered innuendo of the guests around him. He slid the crisp bills into the hand of the maître d' and murmured, "Keep the change."

Still stunned and not quite sure what was happening, he marched for the door. Out on the street he looked both ways. No sign of her. A cold fist of anxiety clenched in his gut. Why was she so upset? Was it really such a big deal that he'd accepted an…investment from her dad?

He shoved a hand through his hair. Of course it was a big deal. She thought he'd married her *just* for the money.

Guilt soaked through him, with a chaser of shame. It had seemed like a happy chain of events, leading to a favorable outcome for everyone involved. But he'd lost perspective on how it had all started.

How would her dad react? Gavin wondered if Elliott Kincannon knew she'd found out. Maybe he could talk her out of causing a big scandal. That wouldn't be good for any of them.

And if she broke off the marriage, Kincannon might demand the one million dollars back.

Gavin stopped dead still, right in the middle of the road. A car swerved around him and he leaped to the sidewalk. He'd already spent a good chunk of the money on the lease for the new offices. And given a deposit to the contractor renovating the conference room. The money wasn't even his to give back anymore.

He marched through the lamp-lit streets. The apartment wasn't far, so he hadn't bothered with the car. He and Bree enjoyed their evening strolls after they went out to dinner or a gallery opening. She knew a lot about the city's architecture and history, and was always pointing out interesting nooks and crannies he'd never noticed before. The city had really come alive for him since he'd met Bree.

A pang of regret stung his chest. How awful that she'd found out like this. He could just picture her overhearing that message. She must have been devastated. If only he could find her and explain that he really did care about her and not about the money.

The elevator seemed to move like molasses on the way up to the apartment. What if she was already gone by the time he got there? He'd have to track her down at her father's house and he didn't relish seeing the old man's face if there was a whiff of scandal in the air. Still, no need to panic, he'd find her, tell her he really loved her, and everything would be okay. He hoped.

He knocked on the door. It was her home too, now. He didn't want to barge in if she was crying.

No answer. He slid his key in the lock and opened the door softly.

"Bree?"

The apartment was dark. He flicked on a light and waited for the sleek shadow of Bree's friendlier cat to appear, but nothing moved. "Faith? Where are you, Ali?"

Dread settled over him like a cold morning fog. The cats were gone, too. She couldn't possibly have had time to come back and get them already, so she must have taken them with her. He strode to her closet and flung it open. To his surprise, he found it still filled with her clothes, most of them new, some with the tags still hanging on them.

So she wasn't gone for good. Unless she had planned to abandon her new look along with him.

A nasty feeling goaded him back out the door and into the parking garage. He needed to get to the Kincannon mansion and win her back. And he needed to get there before the old man heard about their public breakup from someone else.

Usually a slow driver, Bree fought an urge to speed on the freeway. The lights of cars in the opposite lane danced like fireflies in the darkness, dazzling her and adding to her confused state of mind. She slowed down as a light mist of rain blurred the windshield and her phone rang.

Probably Gavin. She wasn't going to answer it. She let it ring and go to voice mail. Then it started ringing again. Again she let it go to voice mail. But the ringing continued and Ali started to mew in protest.

"It's okay, sweetie. We'll pull over and I'll tell that jerk to stop bothering us." She pulled into a gas station and picked up the call, which was probably the sixth in succession.

"Stop calling me, I don't want to—"

"Bree, it's me, Elle."

She stiffened. "What do you want?" It came out just as rude as she intended. Now that she knew Elle was some kind of corporate traitor, she saw her new "friend" in an entirely different light. "Are you going to tell Gavin where I'm going?"

She'd told Elle her escape plan after the party. Before she'd learned about Elle's darker side.

"I still think you should rethink this whole thing." She heard Elle draw breath. "When are you planning to leave?"

"I'm already gone." She said it with grim satisfaction. "I'm on the road right now."

"Still going to Napa?"

"I'm really regretting telling you my plans since I've learned you're a spy."

"What?"

"Don't pretend you're innocent. Brock's detective found out."

Elle was silent on the other end of the call.

"And I'm still wondering if Gavin asked you to give me a makeover so I'd look better on his arm when he married me for money." She was proud of her steady voice.

"He had nothing to do with it. I swear. I do agree that it's a bit mercenary of him to take money from your father, but he's a guy, you know?"

"Well, I don't need one, then. I got along just fine without a man until now. And I'm getting rid of these damned green contact lenses, too." She popped the left one from her eye and tossed it into the backseat. Uh-oh. The world was blurry—which seemed appropriate, but made driving dangerous.

She reached into the glove compartment and was relieved to find her familiar old pair of spare glasses. The second contact hit the floor and she pushed the thick frames up the bridge of her nose. "I think a lot of the *improvements* I've made in my life lately were anything but. And what were you thinking, getting involved with Brock Maddox? It's bad enough that he's your boss, but you're spying on him, as well?"

"It's complicated." Elle's voice was barely a whisper. "I wish I could explain, but—"

"Save it. I've got enough problems of my own." She shoved a hand into her tangled curls. "The worst part is, I feel guilty." She could hardly believe she wanted to share her feelings with Elle after all she now knew, but she couldn't seem to stop herself.

"Why?"

"Because I'm ruining Gavin's pretty little dream-come-true plan to open his own agency. My dad will take the money back and it will all fall apart."

"I wouldn't worry too much about Gavin. He'll land on his feet. These big shots always do."

"You sound experienced in this area."

"Trust me, I am. What are you going to do?"

"No idea." And even if she did know, she wouldn't tell Elle. Here she thought she'd found a new best friend—they'd had so much fun together—and she'd turned out to be even more of a dark horse than her husband.

Husband. What a concept.

"The first thing I'm going to do is have the marriage revoked or annulled or declared null and void—or whatever you do after a quickie wedding. I can't be the first whirlwind bride in California to have woken up in the morning and wondered what hit her."

"I still think you're wrong to give up on Gavin."

"Elle, a man marrying me for money is exactly what I've dreaded since I was a kid. It's not something I can forgive."

"I guess we all have our issues."

"Too right."

"Just don't forget to leave the conditioner in your hair." She could hear a hint of humor in Elle's voice. "It makes a big difference, doesn't it?"

"I admit it does. Has it made me happier?" She let out a snort of laughter. "I think I was better off frizzy. And on that note, I have an escape to make and two hungry cats to feed."

She hung up the phone before Elle could protest and switched it off. Not that Gavin had called. He probably didn't even care enough to come after her. He was probably out there trying to figure out how to save the money—since that's all he really wanted in the first place. He was likely over at her old house right now, glad-handing her father and attempting to turn things around. Who knew? Maybe it would even work. She'd always mattered less than money to her own father, who made no secret of it.

Bree pushed a stray tear from her cheek and wiped a sudden fog off her glasses before she pulled back onto the freeway. At least up in Napa she'd be away from everything and everyone, and could figure out what to do next. Maybe she'd move right away from San Francisco. Everyone here would be laughing at her once word got out. It was bad enough before, being a dumpy heiress. But to be one who got tricked into marrying a gold digger…well, that was more than she could handle. Perhaps she'd just go live in the hills as a hermit.

Hermits could have cats, couldn't they?

Gavin parked his car down the road from the Kincannon house. He could see lights on in the ground-floor windows, but the upper ones, where Bree had lived, were dark. Still, maybe she was downstairs, talking to her father.

He approached the carved front door of the mansion. His muscles burned with the urge to hold her. He wanted to explain that it wasn't as bad as she thought, that he really cared about her and not the money.

The door opened with a creak, and he was oddly surprised to see Elliott Kincannon himself behind it, dressed in a dark smoking jacket, like the nineteenth-century aristocrats he obviously modeled himself on.

"Ah, Gavin." He waved him inside. "How are things with Bree?"

So he didn't know.

"Not so good, I'm afraid." Gavin straightened his back. "She found out about our... arrangement."

"Upset, was she?" Elliott Kincannon led him into the front hallway, over the black-and-white marble floor, past polished wood columns and gleaming oil portraits. "I'm sure she'll recover."

Gavin drew a deep breath. The old man's uncaring attitude irked him. Then he grew angry with himself. Hadn't he also assumed he'd quickly find her and talk her around? Now he couldn't even find her. Panic surged inside him. "Is she here?"

"Here?" Elliott Kincannon swiveled on his heel and raised a brow. "Of course not. She lives with you now. I'd imagine she's ensconced in your palace in the sky."

Gavin frowned at the odd reference to his apartment. No doubt those who owned mansions looked down on those who didn't—even if they knew them to be millionaires.

"We were having dinner at Iago's, and then she told me she'd found out the truth and she took off. She was really upset." Gavin shoved his hands into his pockets. He suddenly hated standing there talking, wasting time. Bree could be headed anywhere.

Kincannon's stare hardened. "She waltzed out of Iago's? I hope she didn't make a scene."

"She threw her rings at me." Gavin took dark satisfaction in telling him this—Kincannon's cold nonchalance was getting under his skin. "Then she stormed out of the restaurant."

Bree's father looked appalled. "People must have seen."

"I'm sure they did."

"Word could get out. The family name might be dragged into the press."

Heaven forbid. How had Bree survived the first twenty-nine years of her life with this man?

"I hoped she'd be at the apartment, but she's

gone and so are the cats. I thought she might be here."

"Well, she isn't. And she'd be most unwelcome if she turned up here. A married woman belongs with her husband. You must find her immediately before a scandal starts."

"I'm trying. Do you have any idea where she might have gone?" A sense of urgency built in his chest. The thought of Bree, out there somewhere, upset and angry and hurting, grew inside him like a hot, uncomfortable flame. "Where does she usually go to get away?"

"Bree never goes anywhere." Kincannon knocked back a tumbler of golden liquid. "Just sits up there with her cats or putters about doing her little charity jobs. That's why I had to go out and hunt her down a husband myself. She was nearly thirty. People were talking."

"Bree's a very special woman." Gavin bristled with indignation at this man's dismissive attitude toward the woman he loved.

Yes, loved. There was no other word to describe the powerful surge of emotion rolling through him.

"Find her and smooth things over before the social pages get wind of this. I can just imagine the gossip if people think I paid to have my own daughter married off."

"Even though you did." Cold fury lashed inside Gavin. He felt like taking the million dollars and throwing it back in this man's expressionless, hard face.

But now wasn't the time for that. He had to find Bree before she got too far away. With her unlimited means, she could get on a plane to anywhere in the world. And then how would he track her down?

"I'll call you when I find her." He turned and marched for the door.

"You'd better find her tonight. If I see any whiff of this in the papers tomorrow…"

"You'll what?" Gavin turned and shot him a confrontational stare. This man was used to rolling over people and making them sweat—and to making his daughter feel inadequate and unworthy. "Bree's the important person here. She's upset, and justifiably so. It's my fault, and I intend to put it right."

If he could only find her.

But he couldn't. She'd disappeared into the misty coastal air. Gavin phoned everyone he knew and quite a few people he didn't. After four days, he was getting desperate.

His college friend Phil Darking was an editor at the local paper, and Gavin even went to see him, in case he'd heard anything on the gossip grapevine.

Phil had the gall to laugh. "Your wife's done a runner and you're calling the papers to ask where she is? Isn't it supposed to be the other way around? What if I use you as the headline tomorrow? It's a slow news day, you know."

"I just want to find out where she is. I've talked to everyone in town. I'm really worried, Phil."

"You think she's going to jump off the Golden Gate Bridge?"

"No, she's far too sensible for that." Why did

people think this was funny? "I love her, Phil. She doesn't know that and I need to tell her."

"You married her without telling her you love her?"

"Of course I told her, but now she doesn't believe me. She thinks I married her for her money."

"Which would be quite understandable. Do you know just how rich those Kincannons are?"

"I don't care how rich they are. I don't care about anything except getting her back. I don't even care about the damn agency I've spent five years planning. I'd scrap the whole thing just to have her here right now, and I'm not kidding."

The realization shocked him. Five years of dreaming and scheming meant nothing compared to the prospect of spending his life without Bree. She'd been gone four long, agonizing days. Four mornings without her smile. Four evenings without her kisses. Four nights without her arms around him. He couldn't take much more of it.

"You've got it bad."

"Tell me about it. I've hired a private detective, I've called anyone I even think might know her, and gone to visit all of her relatives. I've been haunting all her favorite places in the city, but she's just disappeared. No one has even the slightest idea where she is." He blew out hard and looked up at his friend. "I'll do anything to get her back, Phil."

"Anything?" Phil's voice had a funny edge to it.

"Anything."

"I LOVE YOU. COME BACK TO ME."

The bold black print splashed across the front page of the *San Francisco Examiner* on newsstands all over the city. Gavin felt equal measures of embarrassment and excitement as he strode along a crowded street. The air hummed with the zing-zing of a passing cable car and his chest filled with hope. He'd already received a phone call from a popular local TV show, wanting him to come on and tell his story. Much to his surprise, he'd readily accepted.

He'd done the interview that morning. "Yes, I'm afraid I did accept money from my wife's father. I saw it as an investment in my new business." He'd cleared his throat and glanced down at the microphone pinned to his tie. Hot lights had brought out pinpoints of sweat on his brow, and the three cameras pointing right at him hadn't helped much, either.

"Yet you didn't tell your wife anything about it." The heavily starched blonde leaned in until her mascara-clad lashes were almost brushing his cheek.

"No, I never told her. And that's what makes the whole thing wrong. She's my wife and we should confide in each other about everything."

"And she was hurt when she found out."

"She was devastated." Gavin's voice thickened. "After she learned about the money, she decided I only married her for the cash, and that I didn't care about her."

"Is that true?"

Gavin stiffened his shoulders and reminded himself it was a leading question, not an accusation. "Nothing could be further from the truth. I love Bree. She captivated me from the first moment I met her. She's a lovely, talented, sweet, brilliant and funny woman, and I want to share the rest of my life with her."

"Spoken like a man in love." The gruff voice of the male cohost drew Gavin's attention to the side. "And is it true that you've given the money back?"

"Yes. Every penny of it." Pride swelled in his chest. He'd arranged the reverse transfer the previous afternoon. He'd had to throw in a big chunk of his personal savings to cover the money he'd already spent on the new agency. He'd also sent a personal note to Elliott Kincannon, apologizing for his role in the scheme and for any subsequent publicity. Frankly, though, he felt the old man deserved any wind that blew up his well-tailored coattails.

"I'm hardworking and ambitious enough to support Bree without any extra help. I know that now. Whether I can still make a go of my own agency, or whether I go to work for someone else, I'll continue to do my best work for my clients. Since I've met Bree, I've changed my perspective on everything. Work is still important to me, but I've discovered the joys of companionship. I'd never been so happy in my life, as I was during these last few weeks with Bree. I miss her more than I can describe."

"Aw." The female host had patted his leg. "Aren't you adorable? I'd marry you myself if you weren't already hitched to this lucky girl." She'd turned to one of the three large cameras pointing right at them. "Bree, do come back to him, won't you?"

But she hadn't.

Bree's muscles ached slightly every morning since she'd arrived in Napa. Maybe because she spent much of the day walking in the hills, trying to keep moving and keep her mind off a certain scheming and duplicitous man.

Faith rolled and stretched on the sheets next

to her. "Morning, baby." She stroked the cat's soft fur. Sun shone through the delicate blinds on the window and illuminated the pale yellow walls of the pretty bedroom. She hadn't been here in years, though of course it was maintained in her absence like the other properties in the estate. Her mom used to love it here in the summers when she was little, and they often came to watch the grape harvest. As far as she could remember, her dad had never been here, not even once. It was one of more than thirty properties on the family rosters, and he was probably barely aware of its existence. That made it a great place to hide out.

But despite the glorious weather, the lovely surroundings and all the peace and quiet anyone could wish for, she still felt rotten.

And it was all Gavin Spencer's fault.

She heard a noise in the other room. A flopping sound.

She eased out of bed and went to investigate. Something lay on the doormat just inside the kitchen door. Mail? She hadn't told anyone she was coming here. Well, except Elle, but she'd hardly be sending letters. Perhaps people had noticed someone was living here and started to include her on the local "all residents" mailing lists.

It was a plastic envelope from a popular courier service. She ripped it open to find a folded tabloid newspaper. Affixed to the front was a sticky note that simply said, "And turn on the local TV news."

Bree frowned. She pulled the sticky note off the front of the paper and squinted at the large headline. "I LOVE YOU. COME BACK TO ME."

Her stomach clenched and something painful and bright opened inside her.

Ten

Don't get carried away. Bree scolded herself as the blurry black-and-white words danced in front of her eyes. *It's not like it's Gavin talking to you.* Ridiculous that she should even make a mental connection.

Still, something prickled through her—hope, or fear—as she turned back into the cottage and looked around for her glasses. When she found them on the bedside table, her hands trembled as she picked them up.

She pushed her glasses up her nose and

scanned the page. Her jaw dropped as she read on.

"San Francisco is abuzz with the mysterious disappearance of newlywed heiress Bree Kincannon."

She gasped. Disappearance? That made it sound as if something suspicious had happened to her. Was Gavin in trouble?

"She hasn't been seen since last Thursday, when she took off after telling her new husband she'd found out he'd been paid to marry her."

A claw of panic gripped her. How did they know?

"Apparently Bree's father was so keen to marry his daughter off to a suitable husband, he paid the young executive one million dollars to take her off his hands." She cringed. It was bad enough to have such a terrible thing happen, but to have the whole world know...

Tears sprang to her eyes. Who would be cruel enough to show this to her?

She remembered the sticky note urging her to turn on the TV news. Some hidden core of self-preservation told her not to. Did she really want to see herself mocked and gaped at on TV, as well?

She glanced back at the paper. "Since her sudden departure, Bree's husband, Gavin, has been distraught." Bree tugged the paper closer. "Desperate to find his new wife, he approached the papers himself, asking for help."

Bree's mouth fell open. Then it snapped shut. Of course he was. He didn't want to lose the million bucks, so he needed to hunt her down and talk her round before Daddy Warbucks snatched the cash back.

She let out a long, loud sigh and threw the paper down. Even the bold headline, "I LOVE YOU. COME BACK TO ME," read entirely differently in light of the large sum of money involved. One million dollars was worth a little public embarrassment to most people, and obviously Gavin was no different.

Her dad must be hitting the ceiling. He hated publicity. He adhered to the old credo that a man's name should appear in the papers three times during his life—his birth announcement, his wedding announcement and his obituary. Oh, and maybe the occasional impressive business merger. Certainly not a tacky headline about how he paid someone to marry his dumpy daughter.

She would laugh, except somehow tears kept welling up, and now they'd made a big wet patch on the cheap newsprint. Ali rubbed against her leg and she leaned down to pet her. She saw the sticky note where it had fallen on the floor.

"I don't want to watch TV, Ali. It'll be even worse. Why can't he just leave me alone?"

Ali mewed in agreement and wrapped her tail delicately around Bree's calf. Still, curiosity goaded her into the tiny bedroom, to where a small but quite new television sat on a dresser. "I must be a glutton for punishment," she murmured as she turned it on. "Or just silly. I'm sure there are far more interesting things going on in the Bay area than an unhappy heiress running off."

Sure enough, the first channel showed people

chugging some sports drink in a commercial, the second followed the blow-by-blow action of a local prize fight, and the third offered some cubic zirconia rings in a two-for-one deal.

"See? I'm getting an exaggerated sense of my own importance. No one cares about me at all."

Except Gavin. The words snuck up from somewhere in her conscience.

"Him least of all," she said aloud.

Then a thought crept over her. Had he brought the paper himself? Who else would care if she got his message? Perhaps he was out there somewhere, lurking in the rows of vineyard grapes behind the cottage, ready to spring on her and talk her back into his bed.

Never.

She crossed her arms, which were clad in a very unfashionable plaid work shirt she'd found in the closet. Probably from some farm manager who'd used the cottage for a while. These arms weren't going anywhere near Gavin Spencer again.

Oversize cubic zirconia still sparkled on the screen, and she wondered if the ring he'd given her was really an heirloom from his grandmother or a fake he'd bought off the television. When you married a woman for money, it really didn't make sense to throw in anything valuable.

It had been a pretty ring, though. She thought of it falling to the restaurant floor, among stray breadcrumbs and dropped napkins. She still could hardly believe she'd had the guts to do that. Totally unplanned, too! She'd been so upset and angry she hadn't even given a thought to the big scene she was making. It was probably her fault as much as his that the papers had caught onto the story.

The amazing deal on fake diamonds segued into a vacuum-cleaner commercial. Then the local news logo popped up.

Turn it off, now!

Her mind marched toward the set, but her feet stayed firmly planted on the floor.

"Heiress Bree Kincannon is still missing, more than five days after her tearful breakup from her new husband." A hideous picture of her filled the screen. The photo was at least five years old, because she recognized the awful plaid taffeta ball gown her aunt had talked her into wearing to some parties one season. With a goofy updo and a strand of big pearls, she looked every bit the lovelorn heiress.

Ouch. And why was she always an "heiress"? Why not "photographer Bree Kincannon," or even a plain old "San Francisco native" or something?

Her inner monologue screeched to a halt as Gavin appeared onscreen. Dressed, as usual, in a sleek dark suit, heartbreakingly handsome.

She let out a whimper, then cursed herself for it. At least no one was around to hear her. One advantage of being a hermit.

"Yes," Gavin said, leaning into a mike, "I'm worried. She's been gone almost a week. No one has heard from her. Of course I'm concerned."

"Do you think she's extra vulnerable because she's an heiress?"

Gavin looked confused for a moment.

The reporter drew closer. "Do you think she might have been kidnapped?"

Gavin's lips parted in astonishment. "I don't think so, but…" He frowned. "I suppose we can't rule out anything until she comes back. That's why I'm so desperate for word of her whereabouts." He shoved a hand though his hair in that cute way he did when he was thinking. "Bree, wherever you are, please, call me right now. I don't know what to do without you. You're everything to me."

The picture faded away into a story about penguins at the zoo. Bree stood staring, open-mouthed, at the television.

She could almost swear from the look on his face that he meant every word. Her heart beat hard and painful against her ribs, swollen and ready to burst.

"Don't let him do this to you!" she cried aloud. Already he'd turned her into the kind of maniac who ranted to herself. Still, what if he truly did think she'd been kidnapped, or worse? She didn't want him actually worrying about her.

Maybe she should call and leave a message on his phone.

A message on his phone. That's what started this whole mess in the first place. Why did everything have to be so complicated and awful?

The harsh doorbell ring jolted her hard. No way could she go to the door now, cheeks streaked with tears. Even if it was just the mailman, he might have seen the news. She wouldn't be able to go to the store for eggs without people staring. She snapped the TV off.

Again the doorbell rang, harsh and insistent.

"Go away." She hissed the words, not intending for them to be heard.

"Bree." A deep voice boomed into the cottage. It reverberated across the living room and into the bedroom where she stood.

Gavin.

The breath rushed from her lungs and her knees felt weak. *Stay silent. He can't see you here. He'll go away.*

But every nerve ending in her body stung with the urge to rush to the door.

"Bree, are you there? It's me, Gavin."

She closed her eyes and tried not to breathe.

"I miss you terribly." His words echoed through the silent cottage. "I haven't been able to sleep since you left."

She knotted her hands together as his words wrapped around her. She hadn't slept much either. It was hard to sleep alone once you got used to having a warm, well-muscled body next to you.

Remember, it's the money he's after, not you. The icy blast of memory kept her feet rooted to the floor.

"I gave the money back."

Her chin shot up. Had he really?

"I didn't want it anymore. I can't believe I took it in the first place. I was just so caught up in the idea of going out on my own that I didn't think about how it would look to you."

"Because you thought I wouldn't find out." The words flew out of her mouth—barely more than a whisper—before she could stop them.

"Bree, you *are* there!" He rattled the door

handle. "Let me in, please. I have so much apologizing to do." The urgency in his voice tugged at her heart.

"What if I don't want to hear it?" she said weakly. It took all her strength not to rush right into his treacherous arms.

"I'm just so glad you're safe." His relief rang across the space. Suddenly the wall between them seemed too much a barrier for her to bear. Bree found herself walking across the wood floor, silent in her tube socks. When she reached the doorway, she peered around the molding toward the front door, which had two frosted glass panes. She could see the tall shadow of a man—a very particular man—blocking the light behind them.

She stopped. Once she opened the door and got a look at him, she might lose all ability to think straight. "Did my dad demand the money back?"

"No. He demanded that I get *you* back. He's not a man who acknowledges the possibility of failure." Humor echoed in his deep voice.

"I guess that's why you're here, then." She spoke flatly.

"No! I'm here because I want you back. I *need* you back. Bree, I never imagined I could be so dependent on another person for my happiness. Ever since you left, I've been miserable." Emotion reverberated in his gruff voice. "Please open the door. I don't think I can survive another moment without seeing your face."

Bree's heart squeezed. Then she remembered the tear streaks, her unstyled hair, her plaid shirt, sweats and tube socks. "I'm not at all sure you'll like what you see."

"Trust me, if it's you, I'll like it."

"I'm not glammed up."

"All the better. Nonstop glamour was a bit exhausting." Laughter hovered around his voice.

Bree walked very slowly to the door, still not at all sure whether she was going to open it. Her feet seemed to be moving of their own accord with the rest of her going along for the ride. When she reached the door she put her hand on the brass knob and hesitated.

Gavin was there, less than a foot away. She could see his tall silhouette on the other side of the decorated panes, and she could almost feel the heat of his skin even through the wood and glass. Her blood heated and a strange prickling sensation ran all over her. "If I open it, will you promise not to touch me?"

She was afraid of the power he had over her. Too handsome for his own good and far too charming to be safe. He could talk anyone into anything, which was of course how he made his living.

"I'll put my hands in my pockets. Is that okay?"

She swallowed and nodded. "Yes." She turned the knob slightly, and put her other hand on the key.

The click of the latch made her heart jump, and she pulled the door open very, very slowly. Bright noonday light shone in, and her eyes found themselves staring at a white T-shirt stretched over a thickly muscled chest.

Sure enough, his hands were buried in the

pockets of his dark pants. She allowed her eyes to creep up slowly toward his face, up his muscled neck to that angled jaw. Across his sensual mouth, caught hovering on the brink of a smile, to his assertive nose.

Gray eyes twinkled with anticipation. His dark hair was tousled, one lock hanging over his forehead. If anything he looked more gorgeous than ever. The urge to rush into his firm embrace was almost overwhelming….

But not quite.

"You and my father cooked this whole scheme up before we even met, didn't you?"

His lashes lowered in a sheepish expression. "That's true."

"Who came up with it?"

Gavin inhaled, broad chest rising under his white T-shirt. "I'm afraid he did. At first I thought he was joking. I was introduced to him at the gala and we chatted about my ambitions, just casual talk. Then he started asking more and more questions about me—where I was from, where I went to school, what I wanted to accomplish."

"No doubt he was making sure your origins wouldn't embarrass the great Kincannon name." She spoke drily.

A smile tugged at his mouth. "No doubt. I think he liked that I come from a long line of army generals."

"The Kincannons were a warlike people. Some say they still are." She fought her own smile. "So he came right out and asked if you'd consider marrying me for the right sum?"

Gavin looked down at the doorstep. "Yes. Like I said, I thought he was joking at first. Then he introduced me to you and we hit it off. When he and I talked later on that night, he assured me he was perfectly serious and that I was off to an excellent start."

Bree's chest tightened. "Do you have any idea how humiliating this is for me?"

"I can see now that it was totally wrong, but at the time... I don't know, it seemed kind of—old school. Like your dad."

"Biblical, even. A sort of dowry." She narrowed her eyes.

"Yeah." He winced. "Kind of like that. I guess the idea of all that money to start my own business made me look past the more unsavory aspects of the situation." He let out a sigh. "I'm really, really sorry."

Her chest tightened. "Don't be. You're very far from being the only man who might be tempted into marriage by the promise of a million dollars. I guess I should consider myself lucky he at least picked someone good-looking."

The hint of a smile hovered at the corner of his mouth again. "I'll take that as a compliment."

"Oh, come on, you know you're handsome." She twisted her mouth and surveyed him. "That's probably why you were so confident you'd pull it off. You must have women eating out of your hands."

He glanced down to where his hands were still thrust into his pockets. "Not right now."

"You keep them there. Those hands are dangerous." She crossed her arms over her plaid-covered chest. "But I'm glad to finally hear the truth. I bet you were pretty alarmed when you met me. You probably thought I'd be a willowy blonde in a slinky black dress."

"I'm very glad you're not. I prefer curvy brunettes." Mischief sparkled in his eyes.

Something fluttered in her chest, but she resolved to keep steady. "Did you really think, that first night, that you'd go through with it?"

Gavin frowned. "I didn't think all that much. I just enjoyed our dance and knew I wanted to see you again."

"You moved in fast. Swept me right off my feet."

"You weren't the only one getting swept off your feet. I knew right away that you were special."

She swallowed hard. "I prefer the truth."

"That is the truth." He looked pained. "Though I don't honestly know how to make you believe it after everything that's happened. All I can say is that I gave back the money because I realized it doesn't mean anything to me without you."

His words wrapped around her as his gray gaze challenged her to argue.

"But what about your business? Will you have to close it?"

He shrugged. "Quite possibly, but I couldn't enjoy running it anyway if it meant losing you."

She raised a brow. "That's true on one level, at least. I bet my dad would demand the money back if you didn't get me to toe the line."

"It's a moot point now. I don't want it. I'd never take money from him or anyone again unless I earned it honestly." His sincere expression tugged at her heart. "I've been ashamed of myself ever since I realized how much I hurt you. I was an idiot, and I can only hope you find it in your heart to forgive me."

She glanced down at her chest. "I'm not even sure where my heart is, let alone whether I can find anything in it. It's been a stressful week."

"For me, too. I've been utterly miserable without you."

His serious expression almost made her laugh.

"Oh, come on, I'm sure you've been far too busy wheeling and dealing to spend time moping over me."

"I've been far too busy running around trying to find you to do any wheeling and dealing. I was beginning to think you'd moved abroad. It's much harder finding a runaway heiress than a regular person with a job they have to show up at."

She let out a sigh. "Yes, poor little rich girl crying her eyes out at her luxurious Napa Valley hideaway. I guess it's no wonder the press make fun of me."

"No one's been making fun of you, but a lot of people are worried. I've been fielding phone calls from all over the world, some of them less than pleasant. You have a lot of friends."

"I do?"

"Unquestionably. One guy from Colombia was so angry I thought he was going to threaten me."

She smiled. "Oh, that's Pedro. We were in theater club together in college. He's a sweetie."

"And a girl from New York gave me a thorough dressing-down and told me I was a cad."

She chuckled. "That'd be Lacey. She's very outspoken."

"And your aunt Freda…" He blew out a breath. "She doesn't mince words, either."

"So you can't wait to call them all back and tell them not to worry, you tracked Bree down and everything's hunky-dory again."

"Actually, I couldn't care less about them." He narrowed his eyes and stared right at her. "There's only one person I care about." His hands twitched in his pockets, as if he could barely stop himself from pulling them out. "She's right here and she's the most important person in the world to me."

Ali twisted around Bree's legs. "Careful, you're making my cat jealous. I don't think she's going to let you in."

Gavin looked down at the cat. "Come on, Ali, give a guy a break."

Ali stuck her tail in the air and marched back inside.

"Hmm." Bree cocked her head. "That response could be interpreted a number of ways."

"I think she means 'Come on in' in cat lingo."

"Either that or 'Get lost, punk.'" A grin flashed over her face.

"I guess I can't blame her if it's the latter, but I do hope you'll be more forgiving." He glanced down at his hands. "And maybe let me take my hands out of my pockets."

"Oh, okay. Just watch where you put 'em." She gave his bronzed forearms a suspicious look.

"I'll make sure they behave." His hands emerged from his pockets and hung innocently by his sides. "Though I'll warn you, they're pretty darn desperate to wrap themselves around you."

Bree bit her lip to hide a smile. "I did miss you, a little bit."

"Only a little bit, huh?"

She held up a thumb and finger, close together. "Maybe this much."

"I missed you so much it still hurts, even now that I'm here with you."

"I could get you an aspirin."

"A hug would work better." His charming, slightly arrogant grin made her smile and annoyed her at the same time. Of course he expected his charm to work on her.

And of course it did. "You might as well come in. I don't want the neighbors to see you loitering."

Gavin glanced over his shoulder. There wasn't a single house in view. "Good point. The crows might talk."

"We don't want them leaking anything to the press." Her whole body tingled and crackled with anticipation. Gavin's large, masculine presence in the room seemed to fill it and make it smaller. He smelled delicious—outdoorsy and slightly leathery, with a hint of sweat.

She liked making him sweat. "I suppose you expect me to forgive you."

He looked right at her. "I won't ask that of you. I'd rather move forward instead. I love you,

Bree. I know you might not believe that after everything that's happened, but losing you has only made me more painfully sure. I ache for you like I need my next breath. The days are dull and pointless without you. Even work doesn't seem exciting anymore, without you there to share it."

Bree's chest expanded. "That photo shoot was pretty fun." *Even though I was going half-crazy trying to hide the hurt.*

"Everything we did together was fun. Just going out for coffee and a walk in the park, or lying in bed watching the sun rise. I want to watch the sun rise with you, Bree. Tomorrow and every day after that. If you'll take a chance on me again."

His voice thickened, heavy with emotion, and she felt it echo through her. Odd thoughts flickered through her mind.

"I'm sorry I threw your grandmother's ring on the floor."

"It's okay, I have it." He reached into his pocket

again. "I would really like it to go back on your finger."

She noticed with some satisfaction that he was still wearing his ring.

He followed her gaze to his left hand. "I never took it off. I know our marriage got off to a rocky start, but I still believe in us, Bree. I believe in my heart that we're meant to be together."

"Are you saying my dad was a psychic?" She couldn't resist teasing him.

"He might well be. They call him The Guru in financial circles. Maybe his prescience extends beyond spotting the next hot businesses to invest in."

His wicked grin tickled something inside her. "He must be livid about the publicity."

"I'm sure he is." He shrugged. "But I didn't care about him. I only cared about finding you. I'm sorry if the press embarrassed you, but I wanted everyone to know I was looking."

"Pretty sneaky of you to send me that newspaper to soften me up."

He frowned. "I didn't send a paper. I just drove right up and came to your door."

"How did you know I was here?"

He looked sheepish again. She saw his Adam's apple move as he swallowed. "Elle."

Bree blew out hard. "I swore her to secrecy! Of course, that was before I found out she had a dark side. I can't believe she told you."

"She took pity on me. I'm deliriously grateful to her."

"She must have sent the paper. I made the mistake of telling her the town I'd be in. She seemed really keen to get us back together. Why would she care one way or the other?"

"Maybe she just thinks we're perfect for each other." He leveled a wary gray gaze at her. "She wouldn't be the only one."

Bree took in his handsome face, so filled with hope and desire. "Perfect for each other. That's a tall order. We do fit together pretty well, though. Some of the puzzle pieces turned out to have some splinters on them, but I guess we could file them off together."

His gaze darkened and his lips curved into a smile. "I can think of some creative ways to do that."

"I'll just bet you can." She raised a brow. "Promises, promises." Her breasts felt heavy and her belly already rippled with desire. Just being around this man was dangerous. But it was the kind of danger she no longer wanted to resist.

She took a step toward him. Gavin looked as if he wanted to devour her whole. Even with her makeover stripped away, she felt…sexy and irresistible.

"Can I touch you?" His voice was low, breathy.

"Okay."

Eleven

Suddenly Gavin's mouth was on hers, and her arms wrapped around his sturdy back. Bree clung to him as if she would never let him go.

The days of hurt and loneliness fell away as she sank into his warm embrace. Gavin devoured her, his kiss hungry, like a man who'd been starving for days. His fingers roamed into her hair and over her curves as he hugged her tight.

When they finally came up for air they were both gasping. "I've never felt so rotten in my life as the past few days without you," breathed

Gavin. "I knew I was crazy about you, but I didn't know how much until I lost you."

"My head is still spinning." Bree leaned her cheek on his shoulder. "Everything's been moving so fast since the minute we met. I've been so happy and so sad in such a short space of time."

"I think it's time we slowed right down and savored the moment together." Gavin picked up one of her hands and kissed it. "Possibly in bed."

Bree giggled. "I like the way you think." She tipped her head to the bedroom where she'd been hiding from him so recently.

They hurried across the small cottage, anticipation stinging Bree's skin. Already Gavin's fingers plucked at the buttons on her plaid shirt, and his breathing became ragged. Desire darkened his gray eyes as he slid the shirt back over her shoulders to reveal…her dreariest white cotton bra.

"You're so beautiful," he rasped. "And your eyes are so much prettier without the green contact lenses. They're softer and warmer and..." He let out a sigh. "I like the natural you best of all."

He slid the shirt back over her shoulders and caressed her skin as if she was an object of fine art. Heat flared in her belly. Under Gavin's admiring gaze she did feel beautiful. Her whole life she'd felt slightly inadequate and disappointing, until she met him. Under his keen attentions she'd blossomed into a confident woman, aware of her own attractions.

For a few days, that had all withered away. Yes, she'd maintained confidence in herself as an independent person, able to look after her needs and survive without anyone around to care for her. Now, as Gavin's eager hands roved over her breasts and belly, and played in her hair, she morphed back into the desirable woman he'd awakened.

A fine haze of dark stubble shaded Gavin's sculpted cheeks. He looked tired and haunted, but passion flashed in his gray eyes. She slid her fingers under his T-shirt and over his warm skin. "I didn't think I was ever going to do this again." Her heart squeezed. She hadn't fully acknowledged all she'd lost when she left. Now the raw ache of loneliness rose to the surface and rolled away.

"I couldn't acknowledge that possibility." Gavin's hands crept lower, inside the waistband of her gray sweats and over her hips. "Our bed felt so cold and empty without you. All I could think about was finding you and bringing you home."

"You've found me."

"But suddenly bringing you home doesn't seem so urgent." He nuzzled against her cheek, and his stubble tickled her skin. "Because wherever you are feels like home."

Bree sighed. "I know exactly what you mean. I'd never really considered leaving the house I grew up in. It had always been my sanctuary, the place where I cherished my happy memories and maybe even hid from the world. Once I met you it didn't matter anymore. I just wanted to be with you, to live with you and share everything."

Her fingers had found their way to the button of his pants, and popped it free. She tugged down the zipper, urgency flaring in her blood.

Gavin unhooked her bra and pulled it away from her chest, replacing its close contact with his hot mouth. He eased her onto the bed, licking and sucking until her skin buzzed with arousal. She pushed his pants down over his strong thighs, and together they wriggled out of the last of their clothes.

He groaned with raw pleasure as her breasts pressed against his bare chest. He was hard as the brass bedpost and his erection pressed against her thigh, fueling her own intense arousal.

Their kissing became even more fevered, and Gavin was pulling Bree gently onto the bed when the familiar chime of his phone filled the air.

"Oh, no," rumbled Gavin. "Let's ignore it."

"It might be important," breathed Bree. "You do have a business to run."

"Or it could be the press." Gavin winced. "Speculating on where you are."

"The missing heiress." She giggled. "I guess we could tell them I've been found. Though I rather like being mysterious."

"That settles it." Gavin drew her closer into his arms. "Forget about the rest of the world. Nothing matters but you and me."

The ringing stopped as they collapsed onto the mattress together, Gavin's arms firmly around her waist. Bree wriggled against him, enjoying the tantalizing closeness of his hard body.

Then the phone started to ring again.

Gavin groaned. "How can I answer the phone in this condition?"

"But if you don't answer it, you may never get out of this condition." Bree shot a glance at his all-too-obvious arousal. "I could lean over and answer it for you." Bree narrowed her eyes. "But I'm wary about picking up your phone these days."

Gavin cocked a brow. "I'd much rather you answer it while I'm right here so we can talk. I don't want you getting upset and running out on me just when I least expect it."

"Well, when you put it that way…" Bree reached down and fumbled with his pants on the floor until she found the phone. Heart pounding a little, she answered.

A crisp female voice responded. "Hello, this is Lazer Designs. We're inquiring about the address to send the contract?"

"One moment." Bree repeated the question for Gavin.

His eyes widened. "Tell them the apartment."

Bree gave them the address. The voice at the other end said, "Wonderful, and if you could pass on to him that we'd like the entire package—print, radio and television."

"I'll let him know. Thanks." She turned to Gavin. "Lazer Designs wants the entire package."

Gavin let out a whoop of joy. "Yes! I told them the whole situation, about me giving back the money and having to scale back my start-up operation. I even told them I had to give up my lease on the office, which is why they're calling about the address. I guess they decided to go with me anyway."

"They know you're the best." Bree beamed with pride.

"With this contract I'll be able to go full steam ahead. It's a big furniture company with stores in fifteen major cities. They'll keep me busy and fund operations and overhead for a good six months." He turned to her with a smug smile. "Without a penny of your dad's money."

"See? You didn't need it anyway. All you needed was the confidence to go out on your own."

"And you by my side."

"Literally, and figuratively." They lay skin-to-skin on the soft bed. "And I believe we were in the middle of something before we got interrupted."

"I apologize for the interruption." Gavin layered soft kisses along her collarbone. "Pleasure before business from now on, at least for today. I love you. And I'm very, very hot for you."

"I can tell." She whispered the words into his

neck. "And I'm pretty nuts about you, too. I'd have to be to take you back after everything that's happened."

"I'll make it up to you." He nipped at her neck and blew hot breath over it. Sensation flashed over her, tingling to her toes. "Starting right now."

He caressed and kissed her all over as she writhed on the mattress. When she was almost ready to cry out with the force of her desire, he entered her, slowly and carefully, until he was deep inside her. His groan of deep, heartfelt relief sent a smile to her lips. "Welcome back," she whispered. "I've missed you."

"Don't ever leave me again." Gavin buried his face in her neck. "I couldn't stand it."

"Me, either," she breathed. "Maybe we could just stay right here, forever."

They moved together, enjoying each other's bodies until the sun set outside the window. Then they took a break for dinner, before enjoying each other some more.

It was two full days before they set out on the road back to San Francisco.

"I guess flexible hours are one of the benefits of having your own business," said Bree as she loaded her bag into her car. "You can take off whenever you feel like it."

"As long as you're with me." Gavin kissed her and slammed the trunk. "I hate that we have two cars to drive back. I'll be right on your tail the whole way."

She laughed. "That's almost challenging me to try to lose you."

"You go ahead and try. This time I won't let it happen. On a purely practical level, I need you to shoot the print ads for my new client."

"Well, if it's a professional commitment I suppose I'll have to behave."

Gavin frowned. "You never did put your wedding ring back on."

"Does that make me a bad bride?"

"Unquestionably. But since I rather pressured you into putting them on last time, I'll just give you the rings to do what you like with." He fished in his pocket and pulled out the trio of diamonds and the engraved band.

They sparkled in his palm.

"I want to wear them." Conviction unfurled in her chest. With none of the doubt that had given her pause last time. "I'm glad to be your wife and I want the world to know it." She slid the rings onto her finger, where they settled comfortably against her skin. Then she bit her lip. "I need to speak to my dad. Maybe he thought he was trying to help me, but that kind of interference just isn't right."

"We might never have met without his interference."

"I know, but he treats me like a child. Why couldn't he have introduced us and then just left us alone to see what happened?" She cocked her head and narrowed her eyes. "Or would you have lost interest without that initial enticement?"

"Nope." Gavin fixed her with his steady gray gaze. "I knew there was something special about you the moment I danced with you."

A smile crept across her mouth. "The feeling was mutual."

"And you're right. Your dad shouldn't be interfering in your life. You're a grown woman. We'll go see him this afternoon."

Bree gulped. "Well, we don't have to literally confront him…."

"Yes. We do. You do. And I think I do, too. He needs to know that what he did was wrong. That he shouldn't be sticking his fingers in other people's lives. Otherwise who knows what he'll try next? He'll be trying to run our marriage from his downtown office."

Bree bit her lip. "You're right. He has so many ideas about how things should be done. He'll try to pick out our china for us and demand that our children are named after Kincannon ancestors, in the family tradition. I'm named for Briony Kincannon MacBride, born in 1651. We must stop him before he insists on naming our child Elliott."

Gavin grinned. "That would be a serious matter. Let's get moving."

* * *

Back in town they dropped off their bags and freshened up, then set off for the Kincannon mansion. Gavin wanted to get over there before Bree had a chance to get nervous and back out. A phone call to the housekeeper had confirmed that her father was at home, catching up on work in his study. Bree told her to keep their visit a secret, so she could set the agenda for a change.

"He's going to be mad about the publicity." Bree twisted her fingers together as they climbed the stone steps to the mansion.

"He'll get over it." Gavin rubbed her back. "Stay strong."

Lena, the housekeeper, gave Bree a warm hug and almost wept with happiness to see her back. "We were all so worried. The papers said you'd disappeared." She shot a stern glance at Gavin. "You be more careful with Bree."

"Trust me, I will," he said with conviction. Lena rewarded him with a smile, and ushered them upstairs.

Gavin tensed slightly as Bree knocked on the tall wood-paneled door of Elliott Kincannon's office. Bree, however, held her chin high and entered boldly when he said, "Come in."

"Hi, Dad." Gavin watched Bree falter for a moment as her father's stunned expression turned to a dark glower.

"You're back." Kincannon frowned, then rose and rounded the desk. "I'm glad you're unharmed." He shot a dark look at Gavin, who willed himself to remain silent. He could think of a few things to say to Elliott Kincannon, but this was Bree's moment.

She stared directly at him. "Why did you feel the need to pay someone to marry me?"

Kincannon cleared his throat. "I wanted to see you comfortably settled."

"And you didn't think that would ever happen without a financial incentive?" Bree cocked her head, causing her curls to fall over one shoulder.

"You're twenty-nine. I was becoming concerned."

"That I'd be an embarrassment to you." She spoke softly. "That people would whisper about how Bree Kincannon is getting older and no one wants to marry her."

"Of course not. I…" Her father had an uncharacteristically speechless moment.

"I've had offers, Dad. Several, in fact—some from men I'd barely met. When you have money, there are all kinds of people who'll happily marry you just to get their hands on it. If I wanted someone who'd marry me for my money, I could handle that all by myself in no time." She drew in a breath. "I was waiting for someone who'd marry me *without* wanting my money. Someone who was interested in *me*."

Kincannon shot a glance at Gavin, then looked back at Bree. "I imagine Mr. Spencer's gallant gesture of throwing my one millions dollars back in my face demonstrates to you that he is a man of such caliber."

"It helped. We'll never know what would have happened if you hadn't offered him the money, but at least I know he still wants me without it."

Bree took a step toward Kincannon, who stood like a statue, dressed in a fitted pinstriped suit even in the privacy of his own home.

"Dad…" She reached out her hands and picked up one of his. "I really do believe you meant well. That you wanted me to marry a nice man and be happy. I don't blame you for trying to micromanage the situation, since that's just how you're used to dealing with things." She swallowed. "But please, in the future, let me make my own choices and live my life the way I see fit."

Kincannon nodded, his stern face clouded with emotion. "I'll do my best. It won't be easy, though." A smile lifted his wry mouth. "As you've observed, I am used to running the show."

"Well, Gavin and I are going to run our own show from now on. We'd very much like you to take a strong supporting role, but we also look forward to figuring things out on our own."

"Understood." His expression contained a mix

of warmth and pride. It was obvious that he respected Bree for standing up to him.

Gavin cleared his throat. It was time for him to say his piece. "I apologize profusely for my role in the whole financial transaction. I should have refused immediately when you mentioned it. My gut instincts certainly told me to, but—like you—I saw a certain symmetry to the proposition. Perhaps we men are just too inclined to turn everything into a business deal. Anyway, I regret my role in hurting Bree's feelings, especially since I knew almost immediately that she was the woman for me—money or no money."

He looked at Bree and saw tears glisten in her eyes. His chest tightened and he fought the urge to tug her into his arms. "I'll just have to spend the rest of my life proving that to her."

"I have a feeling that you'll prove it very nicely." Elliott Kincannon crossed the room and took Gavin's hand in both of his. "Say what you will, I'm a good judge of character, and I liked you straightaway. I won't say there haven't been some moments when I changed my mind—"

he arched a brow "—but I stand by my original opinion that you'll make an excellent husband for my daughter. I wish you both a happy marriage, and a long one. Longer than the brief years I shared with Bree's lovely mother. I never did meet another woman worthy of my hand."

Bree's tears finally rolled from her eyes. "Oh, Dad, I still miss Mom, too. You never speak about her."

"Still hurts too much, I'm afraid." He rubbed Bree's arm. "A love like that comes only once in a lifetime. I'm just lucky to have enjoyed it when I did." He glanced up at Gavin. "I am relying on you two to give me grandchildren, of course."

"We figured." Gavin winked at Bree. "But we're picking the names."

Kincannon let out a guffaw. "Bree told you about our family tradition?"

"I'm afraid so, and we intend to make new traditions of our own." An idea occurred to him. "Starting today. I'd like to take both of you out to dinner to celebrate a new beginning for all of us."

He looked at Bree for a response. She grinned enthusiastically. "Sounds great."

Gavin turned to her father.

"You're on." Then Kincannon lifted a brow. "But are you sure you can afford it? We Kincannons have expensive tastes."

"I don't," protested Bree. "Our favorite Thai restaurant isn't expensive at all. I bet you'd like it, too, Dad, if you were brave enough to try it."

"Perhaps it's time for me to broaden my horizons."

"Off we go, then." Gavin wrapped his arm around Bree.

She smiled and returned the gesture. He enjoyed the warm sensation of her arm tucked firmly around his middle. "And this time we're all sticking together. No secrets and no surprises."

"I promise." Gavin couldn't resist lowering his lips to hers for a stolen kiss. The delicate scent of her skin overwhelmed him as he pressed his lips to hers. He wanted to hold her in his arms forever.

The sound of Elliott Kincannon clearing his throat jerked him out of the romantic moment. "Save the mushy stuff for later, kids."

"Okay, Dad. We'll do our best. We were apart for nearly an entire week, though, so we have some catching up to do."

"I'm sure you'll manage."

"Yes, we will." Gavin seized the moment to gaze into Bree's beautiful gray-green eyes. "We have an entire lifetime to enjoy each other."

As Kincannon marched past them out the door, they heard the words "Indeed. And frankly I think I deserve a little credit."

But they were too busy kissing to reply.

Epilogue

"I'd almost suspect you of trying to keep me away from our home." Bree eyed her husband suspiciously. After nearly six months of marriage he still managed to intrigue her sometimes. They'd been walking around San Francisco all afternoon, from the Presidio clear across to Fisherman's Wharf, and he kept finding new places for them to go.

"Me? I just want to buy you a new pair of earrings. Is that a crime?" Gavin's gray eyes glittered with amusement.

"You've already bought me a new dress, a pair

of shoes, some utterly wicked lingerie and silk stockings complete with lacy garters. Anyone would think you were trying to dress me up for something."

He shrugged. "I enjoy shopping sometimes. Business has been so good lately, why not enjoy the rewards?"

"I do appreciate the generosity—and I'm desperately proud of your success—but I'm kind of ready to go home." Their new house still needed a lot of work, but already it had become a sanctuary from the bustle of daily life. High on a hill, with its little garden and breathtaking view across the bay, it promised to be perfect—after a few more months of renovation drama.

"Well, if you insist." Gavin smiled mysteriously.

Bree stopped in her tracks on the pavement. "I'm actually allowed to go home?"

"Sure, why not?" His handsome face beamed with good humor. "We can go home and kick back with a glass of wine. It's Sunday tomorrow, after all."

"Phew." Bree hoisted a glossy shopping bag onto her shoulder. Gavin was carrying three others. "I was beginning to think you'd march me around the city all weekend."

"Just one thing first, though. We have to stop by my office on the way."

Brew blew out an exasperated sigh. "I knew there would be something."

"Important paper I forgot." The twinkle in his eye made her suspicious. "But don't worry, we'll get a cab."

Gavin told the cab to wait outside the small brownstone he'd found to house modest offices on the third floor. Once inside, Bree was surprised to find a bottle of champagne chilling in a silver bucket.

"Who put this here?" She touched the condensation droplets on the frosty bucket. "It's still ice-cold."

"Who cares?" Gavin uncorked the bottle and poured it into two flutes. "Let's drink it."

Bree frowned and glanced about. Everything else looked the same. Cluttered desk, piles of correspondence, big leather sofas for clients to wait on. Still, she took the offered glass and sipped. "Mmm, that's delicious."

"I agree. Just what the doctor ordered after a long day of shopping. Now get changed."

"You're very bossy all of a sudden. What's going on?"

Gavin just gave another mysterious shrug. "I'll bring your bags into the conference room so you can have some privacy." He swept up the colorful bags and carried them to the long walnut table.

"Privacy?" Bree frowned, a growing feeling of excitement—or dread—swelling inside her. "We're married."

"I know. Let me know if you need help putting on the lingerie." With a mischievous smile he closed the door behind him, leaving her alone with their purchases.

When she emerged, smoothing her new jade-green dress, a big grin lit his face. "Would have looked better with earrings, but not half-bad."

"Oh, you!" She put her hands on her hips.

"What's going on? Is that cab still downstairs? If so, let's grab him before he leaves. I'm not sure I can walk more than a block in these shoes." She stuck out one of her new suede Manolos.

"Then let's go." Gavin grabbed her by the arm and pulled her down the stairs.

Despite persistent quizzing in the cab on the way home, she couldn't get a word out of him. They pulled up in front of the house. Windows dark in the dusk, it looked the same as always. No sign of anything suspicious going on. "Why am I all dressed up?"

"Why not?" Gavin paid the cab driver. "Let's go inside and relax." He marched up the front steps and she followed as fast as her heels would allow. "Huh. I forgot my key—do you have yours?"

"Sure." She frowned and reached into her purse. Gavin never forgot or lost anything. Yet more to be suspicious about. She slid the key into the lock and turned it. As she pushed the door open, a blast of light filled her eyes, and she saw their modest hallway was crammed with people.

"Surprise!"

Bree might have fallen back down the steps if Gavin hadn't been standing there to catch her. "It's our wedding reception," he whispered in her ear. "A few months overdue, but better late than never."

"Oh, Gavin." Tears welled in her eyes as she recognized the faces of her friends from high school and college, even from nursery school, and her old nanny! All the people she would have invited to her wedding—if she'd had time to let them know about it.

Her father stepped forward out of the throng and kissed her on the cheek. "You look radiant, darling."

"Thanks. It's all Gavin's fault." She wiped away a tear. Then she glanced up. "The walls, they're painted!" She and Gavin had been painting—and plastering, and sanding, and varnishing—for several weekends. He'd insisted on doing most of the work himself and wouldn't let her pay for a thing. As a result the renovations had promised to take most of the next decade. Now, suddenly, everything looked perfect.

Gavin squeezed her. "I got a crew in today. Fifteen guys. They promised to knock it all out in an afternoon, and it looks like they kept their word." He led Bree through the foyer into the high-ceilinged living room, where, sure enough, the walls gleamed with new paint, the exact soft yellow they'd talked about. "It's beautiful."

They greeted friends and talked and laughed and drank and ate a fantastic catered buffet, then danced on the newly paved terrace until the sun started to peep over the horizon.

Gavin caught her and twirled her around. His breath heated her cheek as his strong arms wrapped around her like a cocoon. "Do you forgive me for keeping you guessing all afternoon?"

"I forgive you, my love. I forgive you for everything." Laughter and tears mingled together in a soft sweet kiss that lifted them above the merry crowd into a world of their own.

* * * * *

Discover Pure Reading Pleasure with

Visit the Mills & Boon website for all the latest in romance

Buy all the latest releases, backlist and eBooks

Find out more about our authors and their books

Join our community and chat to authors and other readers

Free online reads from your favourite authors

Win with our fantastic online competitions

Sign up for our free monthly eNewsletter

Tell us what you think by signing up to our reader panel

Rate and review books with our star system

www.millsandboon.co.uk

 Follow us at twitter.com/millsandboonuk

 Become a fan at facebook.com/romancehq